CW00701068

Dear Giles

I don't often have a chance to give you a book you haven't already seen. Here one is — you, of course, published one of the earliest stories.

I hope you enjoy it someday when you feel like it.

Very best
Sincerely
[illegible]

LUNCHING WITH THE ANTICHRIST

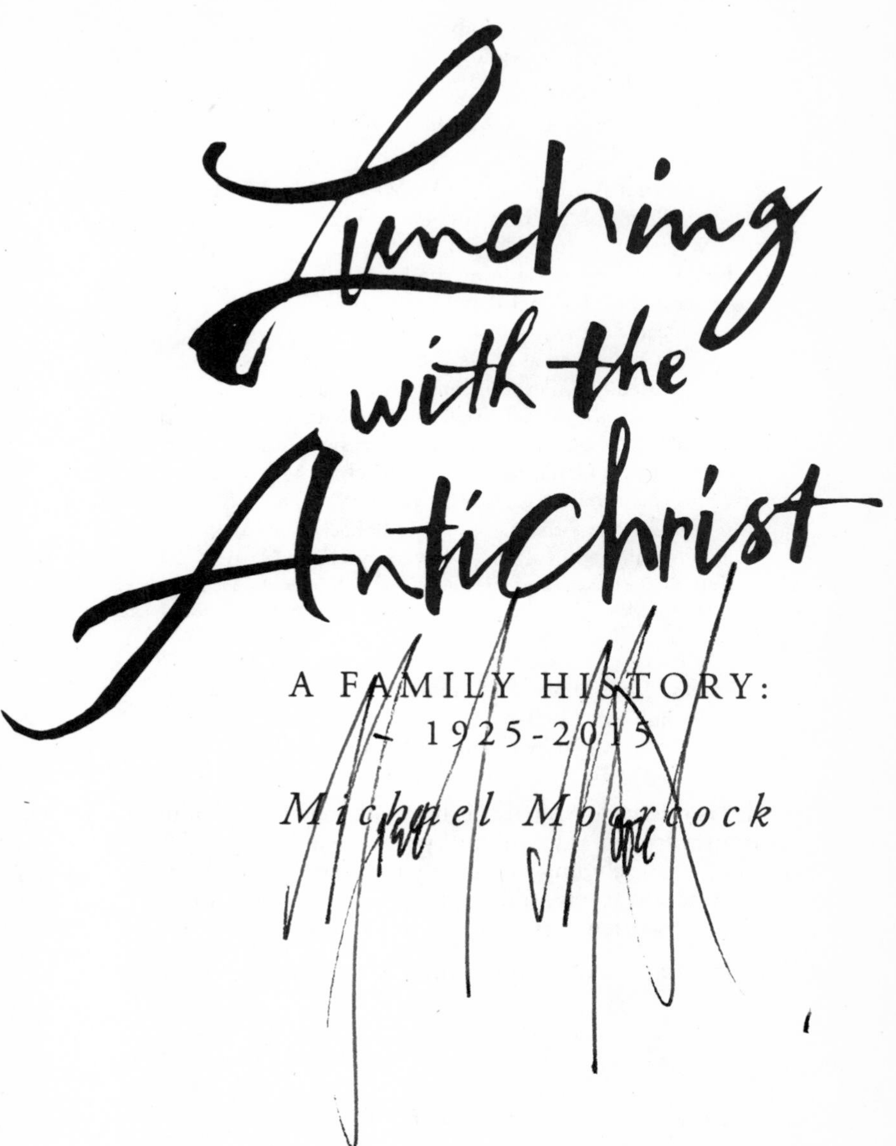

Lunching with the Antichrist

A FAMILY HISTORY:
1925-2015

Michael Moorcock

Mark V. Ziesing

Shingletown, CA

1·9·9·5

Published by
Mark V. Ziesing
Post Office Box 76
Shingletown, CA 96088

The chapter quotes in The Cairene Purse are from poems or lyrics by: 1. Hood; 2. Khayyam/Fitzgerald; 3. AE; 4. Dylan Thomas; 5. Wheldrake; 6. Yokum; 7. Aeschylus/MacNiece; 8. Vachel Lindsay; 9. F. Thompson; 10. Peake; 11. Treece; 12. Duffy; 13. Nye; 14. C.D. Lewis; 15. E. St. V. Millay; 16. Nye.

Manufactured in the United States of America

FIRST EDITION

Design by
Cathy Burnett

Design Production by
Robert Frazier

ISBN 0-929480-46-5 trade edition
0-929480-47-3 signed limited edition
LIBRARY OF CONGRESS 94-061631

CONTENTS

LUNCHING WITH THE ANTICHRIST

For Linda

Introduction

For the past few years I have been writing stories about the von Bek family and its various branches, including the English Beggs and Becks, the Russian Bekovs. Some stories have had supernatural or historical elements, some have been realistic, with contemporary settings. Like the characters from my Cornelius books, the von Beks move rather effortlessly between the various spheres and their experiences are pretty wide, from the miraculous to the mundane. They have descended into Hell and stood at the gates of Heaven. They have been soldiers, housewives, scientists, playboys, politicians and groupies. Yet they have all been people who have sought, in one form or another, a holy grail.

The Grail has occasionally turned out to be a rather spectacular cup with magical properties but more often it has taken the form of relationships, sexual fulfillment, spiritual revelation.

This collection of stories is mostly about people looking for some kind of resolution or meaning to their lives. Perhaps because of their nature the tales possess an elegaic note. I hope their tone does not reflect despair or cynicism, only a cautious optimism in the ability of human beings to conquer those self-destructive traits which distinguish us so painfully from the angels.

Michael Moorcock
Lost Pines, Texas
June 1994

A WINTER ADMIRAL

A WINTER ADMIRAL

After lunch she woke up, thinking the rustling from the pantry must be a foraging mouse brought out of hibernation by the unusual warmth. She smiled. She never minded a mouse or two for company and she had secured anything she would not want them to touch.

No, she really didn't mind the mice at all. Their forebears had been in these parts longer than hers and had quite as much right to the territory. More of them, after all, had bled and died for home and hearth. They had earned their tranquility. Her London cats were perfectly happy to enjoy a life of peaceful coexistence.

"We're a family." She yawned and stretched. "We probably smell pretty much the same by now." She took up the brass poker and opened the fire door of the stove. "One big happy family, us and the mice and the spiders."

After a few moments the noise from the pantry stopped. She was surprised it did not resume. She poked down the burning logs, added two more from her little pile, closed the door and adjusted the vents. That would keep in nicely.

As she leaned back in her chair she heard the sound again. She got up slowly to lift the latch and peer in. Through the outside pantry window, sunlight laced the bars of dust and brightened her shelves. She looked on the floor for droppings. Amongst her cat-litter bags, her indoor gardening tools, her electrical bits and pieces, there was nothing eaten and no sign of a mouse.

Today it was even warm in the pantry. She checked a couple of jars of pickles. It didn't do for them to heat up. They seemed all right. This particular pantry had mostly canned things. She only ever needed to shop once a week.

She closed the door again. She was vaguely ill at ease. She hated anything odd going on in her house. Sometimes she lost perspective. The best way to get rid of the feeling was to take a walk. Since the sun was so bright today, she would put on her coat and stroll up the lane for a bit.

It was one of those pleasant February days which deceives you into believing spring has arrived. A cruel promise, really, she thought. This weather would be gone soon enough. Make the best of it, she said to herself. She would leave the radio playing, put a light on in case it grew dark before she was back, and promise herself *The Charlie Chester Show,* a cup of tea and a scone when she got home. She lifted the heavy iron kettle, another part of her inheritance, and put it on the hob. She set her big, brown teapot on the brass trivet.

The scent of lavender struck her as she opened her coat cupboard. She had just re-lined the shelves and drawers. Lavender reminded her of her first childhood home.

"We're a long way from Mitcham now," she told the cats as she took her tweed overcoat off the hanger. Her Aunt Becky had lived here until her last months in the nursing home. Becky had inherited Crow Cottage from the famous Great Aunt Begg. As far as Marjorie Begg could tell, the place had been inhabited by generations of retired single ladies, almost in trust, for centuries.

Mrs. Begg would leave Crow Cottage to her own niece, Clare,

who looked after Jessie, her half-sister. A chronic invalid, Jessie must soon die, she was so full of rancour.

A story in a Cotswold book said this had once been known as Crone's Cottage. She was amused by the idea of ending her days as the local crone. She would have to learn to cackle. The crone was a recognized figure in any English rural community, after all. She wondered if it were merely coincidence that made Rab, the village idiot, her handyman. He worshipped her. She would do anything for him. He was like a bewildered child since his wife had thrown him out: she could make more in benefits than he made in wages. He had seemed reconciled to the injustice: "I was never much of an earner." That apologetic grin was his response to most disappointment. It probably hadn't been fitting for a village idiot to be married, any more than a crone. Yet who had washed and embroidered the idiot's smocks in the old days?

She had been told Rab had lost his digs and was living wild in Wilson's abandoned farm buildings on the other side of the wood.

Before she opened her front door she thought she heard the rustling again. The sound was familiar, but not mice. Some folded Cellophane unravelling as the cupboard warmed up? The cottage had never been cosier.

She closed the door behind her, walking up the stone path under her brown tangle of honeysuckle and through the gate to the rough farm lane. Between the tall, woven hedges she kept out of the shade as much as she could. She relished the air, the winter scents, the busy finches, sparrows, tits and yellow-hammers. A chattering robin objected to her passing and a couple of wrens fussed at her. She clicked her tongue, imitating their angry little voices. The broad meadows lay across the brow of the hills like shawls, their dark-brown furrows laced with melting frost, bright as crystal. Birds flocked everywhere, to celebrate this unexpected ease in the winter's grey.

Her favourites were the crows and magpies. Such old, alien birds.

So wise. Closer to the dinosaurs and inheriting an unfathomable memory. Was that why people took against them? She had learned early that intelligence was no better admired in a bird than in a woman.

The thought of her father made her shudder, even out here on this wide, unthreatening Cotswold hillside, and she felt suddenly lost, helpless, the cottage no longer her home. Even the steeple on the village church, rising beyond the elms, seemed completely inaccessible. She hated the fear more than she hated the man who had infected her with it—as thoroughly as if he had infected her with a disease. She blamed herself. What good was hatred? He had died wretchedly, of exposure, in Hammersmith, between his pub and his flat, a few hundred yards away.

Crow Cottage, with its slender evergreens and lattice of willow boughs, was as safe and welcoming as always when she turned back into her lane. As the sun fell it was growing colder, but she paused for a moment. The cottage, with its thatch and its chimney, its walls and its hedges, was a picture. She loved it. It welcomed her, even now, with so little colour in the garden.

She returned slowly, enjoying the day, and stepped back over her hearth, into her dream of security, her stove and her cats and her rattling kettle. She was in good time for *Sing Something Simple* and would be eating her scones by the time Charlie Chester came on. She had never felt the need for a television here, though she had been a slave to it in Streatham. Jack had liked his sport.

He had been doing his pools when he died.

When she came back to the flat that night, Jack was in the hall, stretched out with his head on his arm. She knew he was dead, but she gave him what she hoped was the kiss of life, repeatedly blowing her warm breath through his cold lips until she got up to 'phone for the ambulance. She kept kissing him, kept pouring her breath into him, but was weeping almost uncontrollably when they arrived.

He wouldn't have known anything, love, they consoled her.

No consolation at all to Jack! He had hated not knowing things.

She had never anticipated the anguish that came with the loss of him, which had lasted until she moved to Crow Cottage. She had written to Clare. By some miracle, the cottage had cured her of her painful grief and brought unexpected reconciliation.

It was almost dark.

Against the sprawling black branches of the old elms, the starlings curled in ranks towards the horizon, while out of sight in the tall wood the crows began to call, bird to bird, family to family. The setting sun had given the few clouds a powdering of terracotta and the air was suddenly a Mediterranean blue behind them. Everything was so vivid and hurrying so fast, as if to greet the end of the world.

She went to draw the back curtains and saw the sunset over the flooded fields 15 miles away, spreading its bloody light into the water. She almost gasped at the sudden beauty of it.

Then she heard the rustling again. Before the light failed altogether, she was determined to discover the cause. It would be awful to start getting fancies after dark.

As she unlatched the pantry door something rose from the floor and settled against the window. She shivered, but did not retreat.

She looked carefully. Then, to her surprise: "Oh, it's a butterfly!"

The butterfly began to beat again upon the window. She reached to cup it in her hands, to calm it. "Poor thing."

It was a newborn Red Admiral, its orange, red and black markings vibrant as summer. "Poor thing." It had no others of its kind.

For a few seconds the butterfly continued to flutter, and then was still. She widened her hands to look in. She watched its perfect, questing antennae, its extraordinary legs, she could almost smell it. A small miracle, she thought, to make a glorious day complete.

An unexpected sadness filled her as she stared at the butterfly. She carried it to the door, pushed the latch with her cupped hands, and walked into the twilight. When she reached the gate she opened her hands again, gently, to relish the vivacious delicacy of the creature. Mrs. Begg sighed, and with a sudden, graceful movement lifted her open palms to let the Admiral taste the air.

In two or three wingbeats the butterfly was up, a spot of busy, brilliant color streaming towards the east and the cold horizon.

As it gained height, it veered, its wings courageous against the freshening wind.

Shielding her eyes, Mrs. Begg watched the Admiral turn and fly over the thatch, to be absorbed in the setting sun.

It was far too cold now to be standing there. She went inside and shut the door. The cats still slept in front of the stove. With the potholder she picked up the kettle, pouring lively water over the tea. Then she went to close her pantry door.

"I really couldn't bear it," she said. "I couldn't bear to watch it die."

WHEEL OF FORTUNE

Wheel of Fortune

1 : The Hermit

His wife, he said, had negro blood. "It makes her volatile, like Pushkin."

Watching him later, as he played the table, I saw him show panic twice. He recovered himself rapidly on both occasions. He would rap his wedding ring sharply with his right index finger. His hands were long, not particularly thin, and as tawny as the rest of him—a lion, lazy and cruel, quick as a dagger. "Lord, lord," he would say as his wife made her appearance every evening just before dinner, "she is magnificent!" And he would dart towards her, eager to show her off. Her name was Marianne Max and she loved him in her careless way, though I thought it more a mother's affection, for she was at least ten years his senior.

He would escort her into the dining room and afterwards would never gamble. Together they would stroll for a while along the promenade. Frequently I saw them silhouetted with the palms and cedars, talking and sometimes embracing before returning to the hotel and the suite permanently booked to them. The Hotel Cumberland was older than most and cared more for pleasing its regular customers than attracting the new money which had come to St. Crim; it was a little run down but maintained its elegance, its superiority over more modern buildings, especially those revivalist deco monstrosities which had risen across the bay on the French side, upon the remains of the old Ashkanasdi mansion, where the so-called Orient Express brought rich Americans in large numbers.

I had been spending the summer with my ex-wife, who had a villa just above the town, in the pine woods. Every evening I would go down to dine at the hotel and perhaps indulge in a little baccarat.

De Passoni was the chief reason for the regularity of my visits. The man was so supremely unselfconscious, so unguarded, few would have believed him a convicted murderer, escaped from the notorious Chatuz Fortress outside Buenos Aires some years earlier. There was no sign that he feared recognition or recapture. He appeared to live entirely for the day. And there was, of course, no deportation treaty between Argentina and St. Crim.

I had not by the middle of the season found any means of approaching him, however. Every time I tried I had been rebuffed. His wife was equally impossible to engage in anything but light conversation.

She was the Countess Max, one of the oldest titles in Wäldenstein. Her first husband, Freddie Max, had been killed during the Siege, leading a cavalry charge against the Prussians across the ruins of the St. Maria and St. Maria Cathedral. She had remarried after a year, regaining her estates by her alliance with Prince Osbert, the new prime minister. He had died of influenza in 1912, whereupon she had appeared openly with de Passoni, who was already her lover, until the scandal had forced them to St. Crim where they now lived in unofficial exile.

De Passoni had his own money, from his father's locomotive works, and it was this he gambled. He took nothing from her. Neither did she expect him to take anything. Residents of the Hotel Cumberland said they were a bloodless pair. I thought otherwise.

2 : THE NINE OF PENTACLES

When I came home from North Africa, the following spring, my ex-wife told me that the couple had disappeared from the Hotel Cumberland, although their suite was still booked and paid for. There was a rumour that they were in the hills outside Florence and that the Italian police were resisting an attempt to extradite him. His father had investments in Milan and considerable influence with the authorities. My ex-wife became vague when I asked her for more details, a sure sign that she possessed a secret which she hoped would add to her power.

While she was in her private sitting room taking a telephone call my ex-wife's companion approached me that evening. The woman, Pia, knew through a friend of hers that Countess Max had been seen in Florence and then in Genoa. There was talk of her having bought and equipped a steam yacht. De Passoni had not been with her.

I asked Pia, who disliked me, why they should have left St. Crim. She did not know. She shrugged. "Perhaps they were bored."

Returning, my ex-wife had laughed at this and then grown mysterious; my sign for leaving them.

I borrowed her horse and rode down to the cliffs above Daker's Cove. The Englishman's great Gothic house was a shell now, washed by the sea he had attempted to divert. Its granite walls were almost entirely intact and the towers showed well above the water line even at high tide, when waves washed foam in and out of the tall windows, but the great weather vane in the shape of a praying mantis had broken off at last and lay half-buried in the sand of the cove. Daker had returned to England and built himself a castle somewhere in the Yorkshire Dales. He lived there the year round, I heard, a disappointed recluse. The remains of his great garden were as beautiful as ever. I rode the chestnut down overgrown paths. Rhododendrons, peonies, lilac and great foxgloves filled the beds, and the whole of the ground was pale blue with masses of forget-me-nots, the remaining memories of England.

What had he learned, I wondered, from all his experience? Perhaps nothing. This was often the fate of those who attempted to impose their own reality upon a resisting and even antagonistic world. It was both a failure of imagination and of spirit. One died frustrated. I had known so many politicians who had ended their days in bitterness. The interpreter, the analyst, the celebrant, however, rarely knew the same pain, especially in old age. Neither, I thought, was that the destiny of those whose politics sought to adjust genuine social ills, who responded to the realities of others' suffering.

The paths joined at an abandoned fountain, a copy of the Kassophasos Aphrodite. Even though she was half-obscured by a wild clematis which clambered over her torso and shoulders like a cloak, she retained her air of serene wisdom. I reined in my horse and dismounted.

Struck by her similarity to the Countess Max, I wondered if I, in my turn, were not imposing my own fancy on the reality.

3 : THE ACE OF WANDS

I had returned to Paris for a few days. My investments there were under attack from some manipulations on the Bourse which it soon emerged were fraudulent. By careful covering I was able not only to counter the threat and recover my capital, but make a handsome and honest profit from those whose actions might well have caused me considerable financial embarrassment.

Hearing I was at my house my friend Frere came to see me. He had a message from my father to say that he had been taken ill and was in Lucerne to recover. My own business was over. I went immediately to Switzerland to find my father in reasonable health and breathing almost normally. He was working on his book again, a catalogue of the important buildings destroyed in France and Belgium during the Great War. It was to be his acknowledgment, he said, to an irrecoverable moment in our history, when peace had seemed a natural condition of civilized mankind.

My father asked me to visit my brother at our estates. I had not been to Bek since the last family gathering immediately following the Armistice. Uncle Ricky was long since gone to Italy, obsessed as usual, with a woman, but my brother Ulrich, whom we called Billy, was running the place very well. He was most like my father, more prepared than I to accept such rural responsibilities.

When I left Lucerne the summer had come. Mountains were brilliant with wild flowers and the lake shone with the tranquility of steel. The train wound down to the French border first and then traveled across to Germany. I changed in Nuremberg, which always reminded me of a gigantic toy, like the one made by the Elastolin firm, with its red castle and walls, its neat cobbles and markets, the epitome of a Bavarian's dream of his perfect past. I had a light lunch at the excellent station restaurant and was disturbed only once, by a gang of men, evidently ex-soldiers, who marched in military style through the lanes shouting of revenge against the French. I found this singularly disturbing and was glad to get on the train which took me to Bek's timeless woods and towers, her deep, lush fields, so like the countryside of Oxfordshire which I had explored while at Baliol before the war.

Billy met me himself, in a dogcart, having received my telegram that morning. "You've been in Africa, I gather?" He looked me over. "You'll be black as an Abyssinian, at this rate!" He was curious about my mining interests in Morocco and Algeria, my relations with the French.

Since I had taken French citizenship, I explained, I had had no trouble. But I was disturbed by the Rif and Bedouin rebels who seemed to me to be growing in strength and numbers. I suspected German interests of supplying them with weapons. Billy said he knew little of international politics. All he hoped was that the Russians would continue fighting amongst themselves until Bolsheviks, Whites, Anarchists, Greens, and whoever else there were, had all wiped one another out.

I had less unsophisticated views, I said. But I laughed. Ivy-covered Bek came in sight at last. I sighed.

"Are you ever homesick?" Billy asked as he guided the dogcart up the drive.

"For which home?" I was amused.

4 : THE HIGH PRIESTESS

From Marseilles I took the train down the coast. The sun had given the olive trees and vines an astonishing sharpness and the white limestone glared so fiercely that it became for a while unbearable. The sea lacked the Atlantic's profundity but was a flat, uncompromising blue, merging with a sky growing hotter and deeper in color with every passing hour until by three o'clock I drew the blinds and sat back in my compartment to read.

I determined not to go to Cassis where Lorna Maddox, the American, had told me she would wait until she returned to Boston in September.

I had met her at dinner when I visited Lord St. Odhran at the opening of the grouse season, the previous summer. She had told an extraordinary story about her own sister receiving in the post a piece of human skin, about the size of a sheet of quarto writing paper, on which had been tattooed an elaborate and, she said, quite beautiful picture. "It was the Wheel of Fortune, including all the various fabulous beasts. In brilliant colors. Do you know the Tarot?"

I did not, but afterwards, in London, I purchased a pack from a shop near the British Museum. I was curious.

Lorna's sister had no idea of the sender, nor of the significance of such a grotesque gift.

I discovered that the card indicated Luck and Success.

For at least a week, whenever I had time on my hands, I would lay out sets of cards according to the instructions in the book I had bought at the same time. I attempted to tell my own fortune and that of my family. I recall that even my Uncle Ricky had "Safety" as his final card. But I made no notes of my readings and forgot them, though I still kept the pack in my luggage when I traveled.

"She was told by the police that the tattoo was quite recent," Lorna had said. "And that if the owner were still alive she would have a trace of the design still, on her flesh. The ink, apparently, goes down to the bone. The theory was that she had regretted having the thing made and had it removed by surgery only a month or so after it had been done."

"You're sure it was a woman's skin?" I had been surprised.

"The police were pretty certain."

"What did your sister do with the thing?" St. Odhran had asked.

"The police held it for a while. Then they returned it to her. There was no evidence of foul play, you see. My brother wanted it. It fascinated him. I believe she gave it to him."

I knew her brother. His name was Jack Hoffner and he often visited St. Crim. I had no great liking for him. He was a bad loser at the tables and was reputed to be a cruel womanizer. Possibly the piece of skin had belonged to some deserted paramour. Had she sent it to Hoffner's sister as an act of revenge?

5 : THE NINE OF WANDS

It was raining by the time I reached St. Crim. Huge drops of water fell from the oaks and beeches on to tall irises and there was a sound like the clicking of mandibles. Mist gathered on the warm grass as my car drove from the station up the winding road to the white house with its gleaming red roof and English chimneys. The scent of gardenias in the rain was almost overwhelming. I found that I was suddenly depressed and looking back through the rain saw the sea bright with sunlight, for the cloud was already passing.

Pia waited for me on the steps, her hair caught in some multicolored gypsy scarf. "She's not here. But she'll be back." Pia signed for a servant to take my bags from the car. "She told me you were coming."

"She said nothing of leaving."

"It happened suddenly. A relative, I gather."

"Her aunt?"

"Possibly." Pia's tone had become almost savage and it was clear she had no intention of telling me anything else.

It had always been my habit not to enquire into my ex-wife's life but I guessed she had gone somewhere with a lover and that this was disturbing Pia unduly. As a rule she kept better control of herself.

My room was ready for me. As soon as I had bathed and dressed I took the car back to the Cumberland. Almost the first person I saw as I stepped through the revolving door into the foyer was the Countess Max who acknowledged my greeting with a warmer than usual smile. Her husband came hurrying from the elevator and shook hands with me. His palm was moist and cool. He seemed frightened, though he quickly masked his expression and his face grew relaxed as he asked after mutual friends.

"I heard you had gone to Genoa to buy a boat!" I said.

"Oh, these rumors!" Countess Max began to move away on de Passoni's arm. And she laughed. It was a wonderful sound.

I followed them into the dining room. They sat together near the open French doors, looking out to the harbour where a slender steam yacht was moored, together with several other large vessels chiefly the property of visitors. I was on the far side of the room and a party of

Italians came in, obscuring my view, but it seemed to me that the couple talked anxiously while preserving a good appearance. They left early, after a main course they had scarcely started. About half-an-hour later, as I stood smoking on the balcony, I saw a motor launch leaving a trail of white on the glassy water of the harbour. It had begun to rain again.

6 : THE LOVERS

By the following Sunday I suspected some radical alteration in the familiar routine of life at St. Crim. My ex-wife had not yet returned and it was impossible for me to ignore the gossip that she had gone to Tangier with Jack Hoffner. Further rumors, of them disappearing into the interior wearing Arab dress, I discounted. If every European said to be disguised as a Tuareg was actually in the Maghreb then I doubted if there was a single tribe not wholly Caucasian and at least ninety per cent female!

However, I began to feel some concern when, after a month, nothing had been heard from them while the *Shaharazaad*, the steam yacht owned by Countess Max, was reported to have docked in El Jadida, a small, predominantly Jewish port south of Casablanca. They had radio equipment aboard.

I took to laying out my Tarot pack with the Hermit as Significator. I constantly drew the Ten of Swords, the Ace of Wands and Justice, always for the future but the order frequently changed so that although sadness, pain and affliction lay forever in my future they were not always the finale to my life. The other card drawn regularly for the future was the Lovers.

We turn to such methods when the world becomes overly mysterious to us and our normal methods of interpretation fail.

I told myself that my obsession with the Tarot was wholesome enough. At least it lacked the spurious authenticity of psychoanalysis.

That particular modern fad seemed no more than a pseudo-scientific form of Theosophy, itself pseudo-religious: an answer to the impact of the twentieth century which enabled us to maintain the attitudes and convictions of nineteenth-century Vienna. Everyone I knew was presently playing at it. I refused to join in. Certain insights had been made by the psychoanalystic fraternity, but these had been elevated to the level of divine revelation and an entire mystical literature derived from them. I was as astonished by society's acceptance of these soothsayers as I was by the Dark Age rituals in St. Crim's rather martial sub-Byzantine cathedral. At least these had the excuse of habit. Doctor Freud was a habit I did not wish to acquire.

I remained at St. Crim until early September when I received a letter from my ex-wife. She was recovering from typhus in a hospital run by the White Sisters in Tangier. She was alone and had no friends there. She asked me to cable funds to the British Embassy or have my agent help her. There was no mention of Jack Hoffner or de Passoni and the Countess Max.

I chose one card at random from my pack. It was the Wheel of Fortune. I went down to the hotel and telephoned my friend Vronsky. That afternoon his Van Berkel seaplane landed in the harbour and after a light supper we took off for North Africa, via Valencia and Gibraltar.

The machine was a monoplane of the latest type and was built to race. There was barely room for a small valise and myself. Vronsky's slightly bloated, boyish face grinned at me from the rear cockpit, his goggles giving him the appearance of a depraved marmoset. Since the Bolshevik counter-revolution Vronsky had determined to live life to the absolute, convinced that he had little time before someone assassinated him. He was a distant cousin of the Tsar.

The plane banked once over St. Crim, her wooded hills and pale villas, the delicate stone and iron of her harbour and promenade, the mock-Baroque of her hotels. It would be only a matter of seven years before, fearing the political situation in Italy, she gave up her independence to France.

The plane's motion, though fluid, filled me with a slight feeling of nausea, but this was quickly forgotten as my attention was drawn to the beauty of the landscape below. I longed to own a machine again. It had been three years since I had crashed and been captured by the Hungarians, happily only a matter of weeks before the end of the War. My wife, a German national, had been able to divorce me on the grounds that I was a traitor, though I had possessed French citizenship since 1910.

Gradually the familiar euphoria returned and I determined, next time I was in the Hague, to order a new machine.

After refuelling stops we were in sight of Tangier within a few hours. As always, the shores of Africa filled me with excitement. I knew how difficult, once one set foot on that continent, it was to leave.

7 : THE PAGE OF WANDS

The Convent of the White Sisters was close to the British Consulate, across from the main gate to the Grand Socco, an unremarkable piece of architecture by Arab standards, though I was told the mosque on the far side was impressive. Apart from the usual mixture of mules and donkeys, bicycles, rickshaws, the occasional motor car and members of almost every Berber and Arab tribe, there was an unusually large presence of soldiers, chiefly of the Spanish Foreign Legion. Vronsky spoke to a tall man he recognized from before the War. The exchange was in Russian, which I understood badly. There had been some sort of uprising in a village on the outskirts of the city, to do with a group of Rif who had come to trade. The uprising was not, as it had first seemed, political.

"A blood feud," Vronsky informed me as we crossed the square from the shade of the great palms, "but they're not complaining. It brought them in from the desert and now they have a day's unexpected leave. They are going in there"—he pointed through the gate—"for the Ouled Näil. For the women." And he shuddered.

We knocked on a rather nondescript iron door and were greeted by a small black nun who addressed me in trilling, birdlike French which I found attractive. Since they did not accept divorce, I simply told her I was visiting my wife and she became excited.

"You got the letter? How did you arrive so soon?"

"Our aeroplane is in the harbour." I lifted my flying helmet.

She made some reference to the miraculous and clapped her little hands. She asked us to wait but Vronsky said he had some business in the new town and arranged to meet me at the Café Stern in three hours. If I was delayed I would send a message.

The little negress returned with a tall olive-skinned old woman who introduced herself as the Mother Superior. I asked after my wife.

"She is well. Physically, she's almost fully recovered. You are Monsieur von Bek? She described you to me. You'll forgive me. She was anxious that it should only be you."

The nun led me down whitewashed corridors smelling of vinegar and disinfectant until we entered a sunny courtyard which contained a blue mosaic fountain, two Arab workmen repairing one of the columns and, in a deck chair reading a book, my ex-wife. She wore a plain lawn dress and a simple straw cloche. She was terribly pale and her eyes still seemed to contain traces of fever.

"Bertie." She put down her book, her expression one of enormous relief. "I hadn't expected you to come. At least, I'd hoped—" She shrugged, and bending I kissed her cheek.

"Vronsky brought me in his plane. I got your letter this morning. You should have cabled."

Her look of gratitude was almost embarrassing.

"What happened to Hoffner?" I asked. I sat on the parapet of the fountain.

"Jack's..." She paused. "Jack left me in Foum al-Hassan, when I became ill. He took the map and went on."

"Map?" She assumed I knew more than I did.

"It was supposed to lead to a Roman treasure—or rather a Carthaginian treasure captured by the Romans. Everything seemed to be going well after we picked up the trail in Volubilis. Then Michael de Passoni and Countess Max came on the scene. God knows how they found us. The whole business went sour."

"Where did Hoffner come by a map?"

"His sister gave it to him. That awful tattoo."

"A treasure map? The Wheel of Fortune?"

"Apparently." The memory appeared to have exhausted her. She stretched out her arms. "I'm so glad you're here. I prayed for you to come. I've been an absolute ass, darling."

"You were always romantic. Have you ever thought of writing novels? You'd make a fortune."

On impulse I moved into her embrace.

8 : THE QUEEN OF PENTACLES

I remained at St. Crim for several months while my wife grew stronger, though her mental condition fluctuated considerably. Her nightmares were terrifying even to me and she refused to tell me what they involved.

We were both curious for news of Jack Hoffner and when his sister arrived at the Cumberland for a few days I went down to see her. My visits to the town had been rare. In the evenings my wife and I played cards. Sometimes we read each other's Tarot. We became quite expert.

Lorna Maddox believed that her brother was dead. "He hadn't the courage for any prolonged adventure—and North Africa sounds dangerous. I've never been there. Someone killed him, probably, for that map. Do you really think it was sent by a deserted mistress?"

"Perhaps by the one who actually inscribed the tattoo."

"Or the person who commissioned it? I mean, other than the recipient, as it were?"

"Do you know more about this now?" I asked. We sat indoors looking through closed windows at the balcony and the bay beyond.

"I'm not sure," she said. "I think Michael de Passoni had it done."

"To his victim?"

"Yes. To a victim."

"He's murdered more than once?"

"I would guess so. I heard all this from Margery Graeme who had quite a long affair with him. She's terrified of him. He threatened to kill her."

"Why would he have told her such secrets?" A waiter came to take our orders and there was a long pause before she could speak again.

She had magnificent blue eyes in a large, gentle face. She wore her hair down in a girlish, rather old-fashioned style identified with pre-War Bohemia. When she bent towards me I could feel her warmth and remembered how attractive I had found her when we had met in Scotland.

"Margery discovered some papers. Some designs. And a set of Tarot cards with the Wheel of Fortune removed. The addresses of several tattooists in Marseilles were there. And the piece of skin, you know, came from there. At least the postmark on the envelope was Cassis."

"Everyone goes to Cassis." I was aware of the inanity of my remark which had to do, I was sure, with my wish to reject her information, not because it seemed untrue but because it seemed likely. I was beginning to fear a moral dilemma where previously I had known only curiosity.

9 : THE WHEEL OF FORTUNE

Business at last forced me to return to Paris. Dining at Lipp's in St. Germain on the first evening of my arrival I was disturbed to see the Countess Max. De Passoni was not with her. Instead she was in the company of a dark man who was either Levantine or Maghrebi. He was strikingly handsome and wore his evening clothes with the easy familiarity which identified him, as we used to say, as some sort of gentleman.

Countess Max recognized me at once and could do nothing but acknowledge me. When I crossed to greet her she reluctantly introduced me to her companion. "Do you know Moulay Abul Hammoud?"

"Enchanted, monsieur," he said in the soft, vibrant voice I associated always with the desert. "We have already met briefly, I believe."

Now that we stood face to face I remembered him from a Legation reception in Algiers before the War. He had been educated at Eton but was the religious leader of the majority of clans in the Southern and pre-Sahara. Without his control the clans would have been disunited and warring not only amongst themselves but making desultory raids on the authorities. Moulay Abul Hammoud not only kept order in large parts of the Maghreb but also maintained enormous political power, for upon his orders the desert Berbers as well as large numbers of urban Arabs, could forget all differences and unite to attack the French or Spanish.

It was commonly agreed that Moulay Abul was only awaiting the appropriate moment, while the benefits of colonial occupation outweighed the ills, before declaring the renewed independence of the Saharan kingdoms. His influence was also recognized by the British who acknowledged his growing power in North India and in their own Middle Eastern interests.

"I'm honoured to meet you again, sir." I was impressed by him and shared a respect many had expressed before me. "Are you in Paris officially?"

"Oh, merely a vacation." He smiled at the Countess Max. She looked darker, even more exotic then when I had last seen her.

"Moulay Abul was of great service to me," she murmured, "in Morocco."

"My wife has only recently returned. I believe you met her there. With Jack Hoffner?"

The countess resumed her familiar detached mask, but in spite of seeming ill-mannered I continued. "Have you heard anything of Hoffner? He was meant to have disappeared in Morocco or Algeria."

Moulay Abul interrupted quickly and with considerable grace. "Mr. Hoffner was unfortunately captured by hostile Tuaregs in Mauretania. He was eventually killed. Also captured, I believe, was the poor countess's husband. The authorities know, but it has not been thought wise to inform the Press until we have satisfactory identification."

"You have some?"

"Very little. A certain map that we know was in Hoffner's possession."

It seemed to me that the Countess Max tried to warn him to silence. Unconsciously the Moulay had told me more than he realized. I bowed and returned to my table.

It seemed clear that Hoffner and de Passoni had failed in their adventure and had died in pursuit of the treasure. Possibly Moulay Abul and Countess Max had betrayed them and the treasure was in their hands. More likely the answer was subtler and less melodramatic.

I was certain, however, that Moulay Abul and the Countess Max were lovers.

10 : THE TEN OF SWORDS

The tragedy eventually reached the Press. By coincidence I was in Casablanca when the news appeared and while the local journals, subject to a certain discretion, not to say censorship, were rather matter-of-fact in their reporting, the French and English papers were delighted with the story and made everything they could of it, especially since de Passoni was already a convicted murderer and Hoffner had a warrant for fraud against him issued in Berlin at the time of his disappearance.

The Countess Max emerged more or less with her honour intact. The Press preferred to characterize her as an innocent heroine, while my wife was not mentioned at all. Moulay Abul remained a shadowy but more or less benign figure, for the story had been given a Kiplingesque touch by the time the writers had licked it into a shape acceptable to a wide public.

The opinion was that de Passoni and Hoffner had duped the Countess Max, getting her to buy the steam yacht they needed to transport the treasure back to Europe as soon as it was in their possession. The map, drawn on the skin of a long-dead Roman legionary, had become the conventional object of boys' adventure fiction and we learned how the two adventurers had dressed as Bedouin and ridden into the Sahara in search of a lost city built by Carthaginians who had fled conquering Rome. More in fact was made of the mythical city than the map, which suited Hoffner's family, who had feared the sensational use journalists would have made of the bizarre actuality.

I was invited to dinner by General Fromental and his wife and should have refused had I not heard that Moulay Abul was also going to be present.

By chance it was a relatively intimate affair at one of those pompous provincial mansions the French liked to build for themselves in imitation of an aristocracy already considered impossibly vulgar by the rest of Europe. My fellow guests were largely of advanced years and interested neither in myself nor the Moulay, who seemed glad of my company, perhaps because we shared secrets in common.

When we stood together smoking on the terrace, looking out at palms and poplars, still a dark green against the deep blue of the sky, and listening to the night birds calling, to the insects and the occasional barking of a wild dog, I asked after the Countess Max.

"I gather she's in excellent health," he said. He smiled at me, as if permitting me a glimpse of his inner thoughts. "We were not lovers, you know. I am unable to contemplate adultery."

The significance of his remark completely escaped me. "I have always been fascinated by her," I told him. "We were frequently in St. Crim at the same time. She and de Passoni lived there for a while."

"So I understand. The yacht is moored there now, is it not?"

"I hadn't heard."

"Yes. Recently. She had expressed some notion of returning to Wäldenstein but the situation there is not happy. And she is a cold-natured woman needing the sun. You've a relative there, I believe."

"An ex-wife. You know her?"

"Oh, yes. Slightly. My other great vice is that I have difficulty in lying." He laughed and I was disarmed. "I make up for this disability by the possession of a subtle mind which appreciates all the degrees and shades of truth. Hoffner deserted her in Foum al-Hassan. I was lucky enough to play some small part in getting her back to Tangier. One should not involve women in these affairs, don't you think?"

"I rather understood they involved themselves."

"Indeed. A passion for excitement has overwhelmed Western females since the dying down of war. It seems to have infected them more than the men."

"Oh, our women have always had more courage, by and large. And more imagination. Indeed, one scarcely exists without the other."

"They do define each other, I'd agree."

He seemed to like me as much as I liked him. Our companionship was comfortable as we stood together in the warm air of the garden.

"I'm afraid my wife mentioned nothing of your help," I told him.

"She knew nothing of it. That man Hoffner? What do you think of him?"

"A blackguard."

"Yes." He was relieved and spoke almost as if to someone else. "A coward. A jackal. He had a family?"

"Two sisters living. I know one of them slightly."

"Ah, then you've heard of the map?"

"The one you mentioned in Paris? Yes, I know of it. I don't think his sister recognized it for a map."

"Metaphysically, perhaps, only?" His humour had taken a different colour. "Oh, yes, there is a map involved in many versions of that design. I thought that was common knowledge."

"You're familiar with the Tarot?"

"With arcana in general." He shrugged almost in apology. "I suppose it's in the nature of my calling to be interested in such things. Hoffner's death was no more unpleasant than any he would have visited on—on me, for instance." He turned away to look up at the moon. "I believe they flayed him."

"So he's definitely dead. You saw the corpse?"

"Not the corpse exactly." Moulay Abul blew smoke out at the sky. It moved like an escaped ifrit in the air and fled into invisible realms. "Just the pelt."

11 : JUSTICE

My return to St. Crim was in the saddest possible circumstances, in response to a telegram telling me that my wife was dead. When I arrived at the house Pia handed me a sealed envelope addressed to me in my wife's writing.

"You know she killed herself?" The voice was neutral, the eyes desolate.

I had feared this but had not dared to consider it. "Do you know why?"

"It was to do with Hoffner. Something that happened to her in Africa. You know how she was."

We went down to the kitchens where Pia made coffee. The servants were all gone, apart from the cook, who was visiting her sister in Monaco. The woman and her husband who had kept the house for her had found her body.

"She cut her wrists in the swimming pool. She used Hoffner's razor."

"You don't know why? I mean—there wasn't anything she discovered? About Hoffner, for instance?"

"No. Why, did you hear something?"

I shook my head but she had guessed I was lying. Handing me the coffee cup she said slowly: "Do you think she knew what was going on? With Hoffner and de Passoni?"

"She told you."

"The Countess Max stayed with us for several days. She went down to the hotel. She plans to remain there until the funeral. Hoffner's sister is there, too. A bit of a reunion."

"You think my wife was guilty? That she had a hand in whatever happened in Morocco?"

"She knew Hoffner was involved in every sort of beastly crime and that half the Berlin underworld was after him—not to mention the New York police and the French Secret Service. He betrayed men as well as women. She told me he was threatening her but I think she loved him. Some bad chemistry, perhaps. He excited her, at least. The Countess Max, on the other hand, was thoroughly terrified of him. He had a hold over her husband, you know."

"So he forced them into his adventure?"

"Apparently. They needed a boat."

I found that I could not bear to open the envelope my wife had left for me and walked instead down to the Hotel Cumberland where I found Lorna Maddox and Countess Max taking tea together in the cool of the salon. They both wore half-mourning in honour of my wife and greeted me with sincerity when I presented myself, asking me to join them.

"It must have been frightful for you," said Lorna Maddox, "the news. We were appalled."

"Her nerves were terribly bad." The Countess Max remained distant, though less evasive, less cool. "I thought she was brave. To go inland with the men like that. I refused, you know."

"But you believed the map?"

"I had no reason to doubt. Jack was completely convinced. The woman—the woman on whom it had been inscribed was—well, you know, of very good family over there. She was no more than a girl. The secret was passed from mother to daughter, apparently. God knows where Jack heard the story originally, but he made it his business to find her."

"And seduce her," said Lorna in a small, chilling voice.

"He was proud of that. I gather it was something of a challenge." The Countess Max raised china to her lips.

"Surely he didn't—he couldn't...?" I was glad to accept the chair Lorna Maddox offered me.

"Take the skin?" she said. "Oh, no. That was sent to my sister by the girl's uncle, I gather. There was for a while some suspicion of a blood feud between her family and mine."

"Moulay Abul put a stop to that." The Countess was approving. "Without his interference things might have become considerably worse." She frowned. "Though poor Michael's not entirely convinced of that."

I was shocked. "Your husband's still alive? I understood that he had died in North Africa."

"Moulay Abul saved him also. Through his influence he was given up to the French police and is now at sea, escorted back to Buenos Aires by two Sûreté sergeants. He was relieved at first..."

She stared directly back into my eyes. "He saw it."

Although it was not yet five I ordered a cognac from their waiter. I marvelled at the self-control of such women. It was still impossible to guess their real feelings—one towards her brother, the other towards her husband.

There was little more to say.

"The matter's been resolved in the best possible way." Lorna Maddox sighed and picked up a delicate cup. She glanced at me almost in amusement. "You are very upset. I'm sorry. We were fond of your wife. But she would encourage men to such extremes, don't you think?"

I returned to the house and opened the packet, expecting some explanation of my wife's part in the affair. But she had written nothing.

The envelope contained a folded section of almost transparent skin on which had been tattooed a Wheel of Fortune. It had been wrapped around the Tarot card representing Justice. There was also a visiting card bearing the printed name of Moulay Abul Hammoud and on the reverse, in clear script, a few words—"With my compliments. I believe this is morally, madame, your property."

The note was, of course, unsigned.

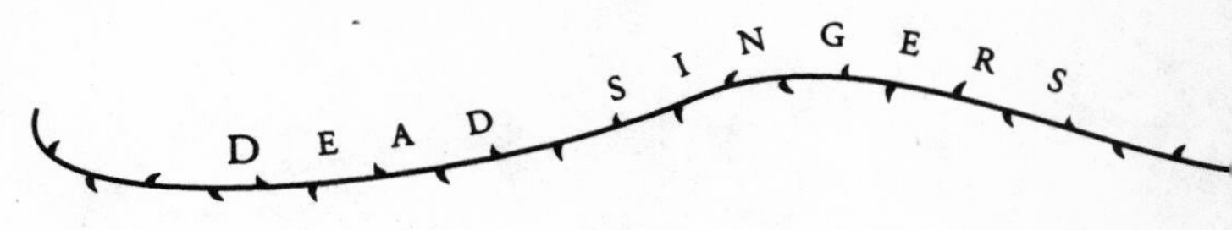
DEAD SINGERS

Dead Singers

CHAPTER ONE

"It's not the speed, Jimi," said Mo Beck, "it's the H you got to look out for."

Jimi was amused. "Well, it never did me much good."

"It didn't do you no harm in the long run." Mo laughed. He could hardly hold on to the steering wheel.

The big Mercedes camper took another badly lit bend. It was raining hard against the windscreen. He switched on the lamps. With his left hand he fumbled a cartridge from the case on the floor beside him and slotted it into the stereo. The heavy, driving drumming and moody synthesizers of Hawkwind's latest album made Mo feel much better. "That's the stuff for energy," said Mo.

Jimi leaned back. Relaxed, he nodded. The music filled the camper.

Mo kept getting speed hallucinations on the road ahead. Armies marched across his path; Nazis set up road blocks; scampering children chased balls; big fires suddenly started and ghouls appeared and disappeared. He had a bad time controlling himself enough to keep on driving through it all. The images were familiar and he wasn't freaked out by them. He was content to be driving for Jimi. Since his comeback (or resurrection as Mo privately called it) Jimi hadn't touched a guitar or sung a note, preferring to listen to the other people's music. He was taking a long while to recover from what had happened to him in Ladbroke Grove. Only recently his colour had started to return and he was still wearing the white silk shirt and jeans in which he'd been dressed when Shakey Mo first saw him, standing casually on the cowling of the Imperial Airways flying boat as it taxied towards the landing stage on Derwentwater. What a summer that had been, thought Mo. Beautiful.

The tape began to go round for the second time. Mo touched the stud to switch tracks, then thought better of it. He turned the stereo off altogether.

"Nice one." Jimi was looking thoughtful again. He was almost asleep as he lay stretched out over the bench seat, his hooded eyes fixed on the black road.

"It's got to build up again soon," said Mo. "It can't last, can it? I mean, everything's so dead. Where's the energy going to come from, Jimi?"

"It's where it keeps going to that bothers me, man. You know?"

"I guess you're right." Mo didn't understand.

But Jimi had to be right.

Jimi had known what he was doing, even when he died. Eric Burden had gone on TV to say so. "Jimi knew it was time to go," he'd said. It was like that with the records and performances. Some of them hadn't seemed to be as tight as others; some of them were even a bit rambling. Hard to turn on to. But Jimi had known what he was doing. You had to have faith in him.

Mo felt the weight of his responsibilities. He was a good roadie, but there were better roadies than him. More together people who could be trusted with a big secret. Jimi hadn't spelt it out but it was obvious he felt the world wasn't yet ready for his return. But why hadn't Jimi chosen one of the really ace roadies? Everything had to be prepared for the big gig. Maybe at Shea Stadium or the Albert Hall or the Paris Olympia? Anyway, some classic venue. Or at a festival? A special festival celebrating the resurrection. Woodstock or Glastonbury. Probably something new altogether, some new holy place. India, maybe? Jimi would say when the time came. After Jimi had contacted him and told him where to be picked up, Mo had soon stopped asking questions. With all his old gentleness, Jimi had turned the questions aside. He had been kind, but it was clear he hadn't wanted to answer.

Mo respected that.

The only really painful request Jimi had made was that Mo stop playing his old records, including *Hey, Joe!* the first single. Previously there hadn't been a day when Mo hadn't put something of Jimi's on. In his room in Lancaster Road, in the truck when he was roading for Light and later The Deep Fix, even when he'd gone to the House during his short-lived conversion to Scientology he'd been able to plug his earbead into his cassette player for an hour or so. While Jimi's physical presence made up for a lot and stopped the worst of the withdrawal symptoms, it was still difficult. No amount of mandrax, speed or booze could counter his need for the music and, consequently, the shakes were getting just a little bit worse each day. Mo sometimes felt that he was paying some kind of price for Jimi's trust in him. That was good karma so he didn't mind. He was used to the shakes anyway. You could get used to anything. He looked at his sinewy, tattooed arms stretched before him, the hands gripping the steering wheel. The world snake was wriggling again. Black, red, and green, it coiled slowly down his skin, round his wrist and began to inch towards his elbow. He fixed his eyes back on the road.

CHAPTER TWO

Jimi had fallen into a deep sleep. He lay along the seat behind Mo, his head resting on the empty guitar case. He was breathing heavily, almost as if something were pressing down on his chest.

The sky ahead was wide and pink. In the distance was a line of blue hills. Mo was tired. He could feel the old paranoia creeping in. He took a fresh joint from the ledge and lit it, but he knew that dope wouldn't do a lot of good. He needed a couple of hours sleep himself.

Without waking Jimi, Mo pulled the truck into the side of the road, near a wide, shallow river full of flat, white limestone rocks. He opened his door and climbed slowly to the grass. He wasn't sure where they were, maybe somewhere in Yorkshire. There were hills all around. It was a mild autumn morning but Mo felt cold. He clambered down to the bank and knelt there, cupping his hands in the clear water, sucking up the river. He stretched out and put his tattered straw hat over his face. It was a very heavy scene at the moment. Maybe that was why it was taking Jimi so long to get it together.

Mo felt much better when he woke up. It must have been noon. The sun was hot on his skin. He took a deep breath of the rich air and cautiously removed his hat from his face. The black Mercedes camper with its chrome trimming was still on the grass near the road. Mo's mouth felt dry. He had another drink of water and rose, shaking the silver drops from his brown fingers. He trudged slowly to the truck, pulled back the door and looked over the edge of the driver's seat. Jimi wasn't there, but sounds came from behind the partition. Mo climbed across the two front seats and slid open the connecting door. Jimi sat on one of the beds. He had erected the table and was drawing in a big red notebook. His smile was remote as Mo entered.

"Sleep good?" he asked.

Mo nodded. "I needed it."

"Sure," said Jimi. "Maybe I ought to do a little driving."

"It's okay. Unless you want to make better time."

"No."

"I'll get some breakfast," said Mo. "Are you hungry?"

Jimi shook his head. All through the summer, since he had left the flying boat and got into the truck beside Mo, Jimi appeared to have eaten nothing. Mo cooked himself some sausages and beans on the little Calor stove, opening the back door so that the smell wouldn't fill the camper. "I might go for a swim," he said as he brought his plate to the table and sat as far away from Jimi as possible, so as not to disturb him.

"Okay," said Jimi, absorbed in his drawing.

"What you doing? Looks like a comic strip. I'm really into comics."

Jimi shrugged. "Just doodling, man. You know."

Mo finished his food. "I'll get some comics next time we stop on the motorway. Some of the new ones are really far out, you know."

"Yeah?" Jimi's smile was sardonic.

"Really far out. Cosmic wars, time warps. All the usual stuff but different, you know. Better. Bigger. More spectacular. Sensational, man. Oh, you want to see them. I'll get some."

"Too much," said Jimi distantly but it was obvious he hadn't been listening. He closed the notebook and sat back against the vinyl cushions, folding his arms across his white silk chest. As it occurred to him that he might have hurt Mo's feelings, he added: "Yeah, I used to be into comics a lot. You seen the Jap kind? Big fat books. Oh, man—they are *really* far out. Kids burning. Rape. All that stuff." He laughed shaking his head. "Oh, man!"

"Yeah?" Mo laughed hesitantly.

"Right!" Jimi went to the door, placing a hand either side of the frame and looking into the day. "Where are we, Mo? It's a little like Pennsylvania. The Delaware Valley. Ever been there?"

"Never been to the States."

"Is that right?"

"Somewhere in Yorkshire, I think. Probably north of Leeds. That could be the Lake District over there."

"Is that where I came through?"

"Derwentwater."

"Well, well." Jimi chuckled.

Jimi was livelier today. Maybe it was taking him time to store up all the energy he'd need when he finally decided to reveal himself to the world. Their driving had been completely at random. Jimi had let Mo decide where to go. They had been all over Wales, the Peaks, the West Country, most parts of the Home Counties, everywhere except London. Jimi had been reluctant to go to London. It was obvious why. Bad memories. Mo had been into town a few times, leaving the Mercedes and Jimi in a suburban layby and walking and hitching into London to get his mandies and his speed. When he could he scored some coke. He liked to get behind a snort or two once in a while. In Finch's on the corner of Portobello Road he'd wanted to tell his old mates about Jimi, but Jimi had said to keep quiet about it, so when people had asked him what he was doing, where he was living these days, he'd had to give some vague answers. There was no problem about money. Jimi didn't have any but Mo had got a lot selling the white Dodge convertible. The Deep Fix had given it to him after they'd stopped going on the road. And there was a big bag of dope in the truck, too. Enough to last two people for months, though Jimi didn't seem to have any taste for that, either.

Jimi came back into the gloom of the truck. "What d'you say we get on the road again?"

Mo took his plate, knife and fork down to the river, washed them and stashed them back in the locker. He got into the driver's seat and turned the key. The Wankel engine started at once. The Mercedes pulled smoothly away, still heading north, bumping off the grass and back on to the asphalt. They were on a narrow road suitable only for one way traffic, but there was nobody behind them and nobody ahead of them until they left this road and turned on to the A65, making for Kendal.

"You don't mind the Lake District?" Mo asked.

"Suits me," said Jimi. "I'm the mad Gull Warrior, man." He smiled. "Maybe we should make for the ocean?"

"It's not far from here." Mo pointed west. "Morecambe Bay?"

CHAPTER THREE

The cliff tops were covered in turf as smooth as a fairway. Below them the sea sighed. Jimi and Mo were in good spirits, looning around like kids.

In the distance, round the curve of the bay, were the towers and fun-fairs and penny arcades of Morecambe, but here it was deserted and still, apart from the occasional yelp of a gull.

Mo laughed, then cried out nervously as Jimi danced so near to the cliff edge it seemed he'd fall over.

"Take it easy, Jimi."

"Shit, man. They can't kill me."

He had a broad, euphoric smile on his face and he looked really healthy. "They can't kill Jimi, man!"

Mo remembered him on stage. In total command. Moving through the strobes, his big guitar stuck out in front of him, pointing at each individual member of the audience, making each kid feel that he was in personal touch with Jimi.

"Right!" Mo began to giggle.

Jimi hovered on the edge, still flapping his outstretched arms. "I'm the boy they boogie to. Oh, man! There ain't nothing they can do to me!"

"Right!"

Jimi came zooming round and flung himself down on the turf

next to Mo. He was panting. He was grinning. "It's coming back, Mo. All fresh and new."

Mo nodded, still giggling.

"I just know it's there, man."

Mo looked up. The gulls were everywhere. They were screaming. They took on the aspect of an audience. He hated them. They were so thick in the sky now.

"Don't let them fucking feathers stick in your throat," said Mo, suddenly sullen. He got up and returned to the truck.

"Mo. What's the matter with you, man?"

Jimi was concerned as ever, but that only brought Mo down more. It was Jimi's kindness which had killed him the first time. He'd been polite to everyone. He couldn't help it. Really hung-up people had got off on him. And they'd drained Jimi dry.

"They'll screw you again, man," said Mo. "I know they will. Every time. There isn't a thing you can do about it. No matter how much energy you build up, you know, they'll still suck it out of you and moan for more. They want your blood, man. They want your sperm and your bones and your flesh, man. They'll take you, man. They'll eat you up again."

"No. I'll—no, not this time."

"Sure." Mo sneered.

"Man, are you trying to bring me down."

Mo began to twitch. "No. But..."

"Don't worry, man, okay?" Jimi's voice was soft and assured.

"I can't put it into words, Jimi. It's this, sort of, premonition, you know."

"What good did words ever do for anybody?" Jimi laughed his old, deep laugh. "You are crazy, Mo. Come on, let's get back in the truck. Where do you want to head for?"

But Mo couldn't reply. He sat at the steering wheel and stared through the windscreen at the sea and the gulls.

Jimi was conciliatory. "Look, Mo, I'll stay cool, right? I'll take it easy, or maybe you think I don't need you?"

Mo didn't know why he was so down all of a sudden.

"Mo, you go with me, wherever I go," said Jimi.

CHAPTER FOUR

Outside Carlisle they saw a hitchhiker, a young guy who looked really wasted. He was leaning on a signpost. He had enough energy to raise his hand. Mo thought they should stop for him. Jimi said: "If you want to," and went into the back of the truck, closing the door as Mo pulled in for the hitchhiker.

Mo said: "Where you going?"

The hitchhiker said: "What about Fort William, man?"

Mo said: "Get in."

The hitchhiker said his name was Chris. "You with a band, man?" He glanced round the cabin at the old stickers and the stereo, at Mo's tattoos, his faded face-paint, his Cawthorn T-shirt, his beaded jacket, his worn jeans with washed-out patches on them, the leather cowboy boots which Mo had bought at the Emperor of Wyoming in Notting Hill Gate last year.

"Used to road for The Deep Fix," said Mo.

The hitchhiker's eyes were sunken and the sockets were red. His thick black hair was long and hung down to his pale face. He wore a torn Wrangler denim shirt, a dirty white Levi jacket and both legs of his jeans had holes in the knees. He had moccasins on his feet. He was nervous and eager. But he didn't know the band.

"Yeah?"

"Right," said Mo.

"What's in the back?" Chris turned to look at the door. "Gear?"

"You could say that."

"I've been hitching for three days, night and day," said Chris. He had an oil-and weather-stained khaki pack on his lap.

"D'you mind if I get some kip some time?"

"No," said Mo. There was a service station ahead. He decided to pull in and fill the Merc up. By the time he reached the pumps Chris was asleep.

As he waited to get back into the traffic, Mo crammed his mouth full of pills. Some of them fell from his hand on to the floor. He didn't bother to pick them up. He was feeling bleak.

Chris woke when they were going through Glasgow.

"Is this Glasgow?"

Mo nodded. He couldn't keep the paranoia down. He glared at the cars ahead as they moved slowly through the streets. Every window of every shop had a big steel mesh grill on it. The pubs were like bunkers. He was really pissed off without knowing why.

"Where you going yourself?" Chris asked.

"Fort William?"

"Lucky for me. Know where I can score any grass in Fort William?"

Mo reached forward and pushed a tobacco tin along the edge towards the hitchhiker. "You can have that."

Chris took the tin and opened it. "Far out! You mean it? And the skins?"

"Sure," said Mo. He hated Chris, he hated everybody. He knew the mood would pass.

"Oh, wow! Thanks, man." Chris put the tin in his pack.

"I'll roll one when we're out of the city, okay?"

"Okay."

"Who are you working for now?" said Chris. "A band?"

"No."

"You on holiday?"

The kid was too speedy. Probably it was just his lack of sleep. "Sort of," he said.

"Me, too. Well, it started like that. I'm at university. Exeter. Or was. I decided to drop out I'm not going back to that shit heap. One term was enough for me. I thought of heading for the Hebrides. Someone I know's living in a commune out there, on one of the islands. They got their own sheep, goats, a cow. Nobody getting off on them. You know. Really free. It seems okay to me."

Mo nodded.

Chris pushed back his black, greasy hair. "I mean compare something like that with a place like this. How do people stand it, man. Fucking hell."

Mo didn't answer. He moved forward, changing gear as the lights changed.

"Amazing," said Chris. He saw the case of cartridges at his feet. "Can I play some music?"

"Go ahead," said Mo.

Chris picked out an old album, *Who's Next.* He tried to slide it into the slot the wrong way round. Mo took it from his hand and put it in the right way. He felt better when the music started. He noticed, out of the corner of his eye, that Chris tried to talk for a while before he realized he couldn't be heard.

Mo let the tape play over and over again as they drove away from Glasgow. Chris rolled joints and Mo smoked a little, beginning to get on top of his paranoia. By about four in the afternoon, he was feeling better and he switched off the stereo. They were driving beside Loch Lomond. The bracken was turning brown and shone like brass where the sun touched it. Chris had fallen asleep again, but he woke up as the music stopped. "Far out." He dug the scenery. "Fucking far out." He wound his window down. "This is the first time I've been to Scotland."

"Yeah?" said Mo.

"How long before we reach Fort William, man?"

"A few hours. Why are you heading for Fort William?"

"I met this chick. She comes from there. Her old man's a chemist or something."

Mo said softly, on impulse: "Guess who I've got in the back."

"A chick?"

"No."

"Who?"

"Jimi Hendrix."

Chris's jaw dropped. He looked at Mo and snorted, willing to join in the joke. "No? Really? Hendrix, eh? What is it, a refrigerated truck?" He was excited by the fantasy. "You think if we thaw him out he'll play something for us?" He shook his head, grinning.

"He is sitting in the back there. Alive. I'm roading for him."

"Really?"

"Yeah."

"Fantastic." Chris was half convinced. Mo laughed. Chris looked at the door. After that, he was silent for a while.

Something like a half an hour later, he said: "Hendrix was the best, you know. He was the king, man. Not just the music, but the style, too. Everything. I couldn't believe it when I heard he died. I still can't believe it, you know."

"Sure," said Mo. "Well, he's back."

"Yeah?" Again Chris laughed uncertainly. "In there? Can I see him?"

"He's not ready, yet."

"Sure," said Chris.

It was dark when they reached Fort William. Chris staggered down from the truck. "Thanks, man. That's really nice, you know. Where are you staying?"

"I'm moving on," said Mo. "See you."

"Yeah. See you." Chris still had that baffled look on his face.

Mo smiled to himself as he started the camper, heading for Oban. Once they were moving the door opened and Jimi clambered over the seats to sit beside him.

"You told that kid about me?"

"He didn't believe me," said Mo.

Jimi shrugged.

It began to rain again.

CHAPTER FIVE

They lay together in the damp heather looking out over the hills. There was nobody for miles; no roads, towns or houses. The air was still and empty save for a hawk drifting so high above them it was almost out of sight.

"This'll do, eh?" said Mo. "It's fantastic."

Jimi smiled gently. "It's nice," he said.

Mo took a Mars Bar from his pocket and offered it to Jimi who shook his head. Mo began to eat the Mars Bar.

"What d'you think I am, man?" said Jimi.

"How d'you mean?"

"Devil or angel? You know."

"You're Jimi," said Mo. "That's good enough for me, man."

"Or just a ghost," said Jimi. "Maybe I'm just a ghost."

Mo began to shake. "No," he said.

"Or a killer?" Jimi got up and struck a pose. "The Sonic Assassin. Or the messiah, maybe." He laughed. "You wanna hear my words of wisdom?"

"That's not what it's about," said Mo, frowning. "Words. You just have to be there, Jimi. On the stage. With your guitar. You're above all that stuff—all the hype. Whatever you do—it's right, you know."

"If you say so, Mo." Jimi was on some kind of downer. He lowered himself to the heather and sat there cross-legged, smoothing his white jeans, picking mud off his black patent-leather boots. "What is all this *Easy Rider* crap anyway? What are we doing here?"

"You didn't like *Easy Rider*?" Mo was astonished.

"The best thing since *Lassie Come Home.*" Jimi shrugged. "All it ever proved was that Hollywood could still turn 'em out, you know. They got a couple of fake freaks and made themselves a lot of money. A rip off, man. And the kids fell for it. What does that make me?"

"You never ripped anybody off, Jimi."

"Yeah? How d'you know?"

"Well, you never did."

"All that low energy shit creeping in everywhere. Things are bad." Jimi had changed the subject, making a jump Mo couldn't follow. "People all over the Grove playing nothing but fake fifties crap, Simon and Garfunkel. Jesus Christ! Was it ever worth doing?"

"Things go in waves. You can't be up the whole time."

"Sure," Jimi sneered. "This one's for all the soldiers fighting in Chicago. And Milwaukee. And New York...And Vietnam. Down with War and Pollution. What was that all about?"

"Well..." Mo swallowed the remains of the Mars Bar. "Well—it's important, man. I mean, all those kids getting killed."

"While we made fortunes. And came out with a lot of sentimental shit. That's where we were wrong. You're either in the social conscience business or show business. You're just foolish if you think you can combine them like that."

"No, man. I mean, you can say things which people will hear."

"You say what your audience wants. A Frank Sinatra audience gets their shit rapped back to them by Frank Sinatra. Jimi Hendrix gives a Jimi Hendrix audience what they want to hear. Is that what I want to get back into?"

But Mo had lost him. Mo was watching the tattoos crawl up his arms. He said vaguely: "You need different music for different moods. There's nothing wrong with the New Riders, say, if you're trying to get off some paranoia trip. And you get up on Hendrix. That's what it's like. Like uppers and downers, you know."

"Okay," said Jimi. "You're right. But it's the other stuff that's stupid. Why do they always want you to keep saying things? If you're just a musician that's all you should have to be. When you're playing a gig, anyway, or making a record. Anything else should come out of that. If you wanna do benefits, free concerts, okay. But your opinions should be private. They want to turn us into politicians."

"I tol' you," said Mo, staring intensely at his arms. "Nobody asks that. You do what you want to do."

"Nobody asks it, but you always feel you got to give it to 'em." Jimi rolled over and lay on his back, scratching his head. "Then you blame them for it."

"Not everyone thinks they owe anything to anyone," said Mo mildly as his skin undulated over his flesh.

"Maybe that's it," said Jimi. "Maybe that's what kills you. Jesus Christ. Psychologically, man, you know, that means you must be in one hell of a mess. Jesus Christ. That's suicide, man. Creepy."

"They killed you," said Mo.

"No, man. It was suicide."

Mo watched the world snake crawl. Could this Hendrix be an imposter?

CHAPTER SIX

"So what you going to do, then?" said Mo. They were on the road to Skye and running low on fuel.

"I was a cunt to come back," said Jimi. "I thought I had some kind of duty."

Mo shrugged. "Maybe you have, you know."

"And maybe I haven't."

"Sure." Mo saw a filling station ahead. The gauge read Empty and a red light was flashing on the panel. It always happened like that. He'd hardly ever been stranded. He glanced in the mirror and saw his own mad eyes staring back at him. Momentarily he wondered if he should turn the mirror a little to see if Jimi's reflection was there too. He pushed the thought away. More paranoia. He had to stay on top of it.

While the attendant was filling the truck, Mo went to the toilet. Among the more common bits of graffiti on the wall was the slogan "Hawkwind is Ace." Maybe Jimi was right. Maybe his day was over and he should have stayed dead. Mo felt miserable. Hendrix had been his only hero. He did up his flies and the effort drained off the last of his energy. He staggered against the door and began to slide down towards the messy floor. His mouth was dry; his heart was thumping very fast. He tried to remember how many pills he'd swallowed recently. Maybe he was about to O.D.

He put his hands up to the door-handle and hauled himself to his feet. He bent over the lavatory bowl and shoved his finger down his throat. Everything was moving. The bowl was alive. A greedy mouth tried to swallow him. The walls heaved and moved in on him. He heard a whistling noise. Nothing came up. He stopped trying to vomit, turned, steadied himself as best as he could, brushed aside the little white stick men who tried to grab at him, dragged the door open and plunged through. Outside, the attendant was putting the cap back on the tank. He wiped his big hands on a piece of rag and put the rag back into his overalls, saying something. Mo found some money in his back pocket and gave it to him. He heard a voice.

"You okay, laddie?"

The man had offered him a look of genuine concern.

Mo mumbled something and clambered into the cab.

The man ran up as Mo started the engine, waving money and green stamps.

"What?" said Mo. He managed to wind the window down. The man's face changed to a malevolent devil's mask. Mo knew enough not to worry about it. "What?"

He thought he heard the attendant say: "Your friend's already paid."

"That's right, man," said Jimi from beside him.

"Keep it," said Mo. He had to get on the road quickly. Once he was driving he would be more in control of himself. He fumbled a cartridge at random from the case. He jammed it into the slot. The tape started halfway through a Stones album. Jagger singing *Let It Bleed* had a calming effect on Mo. The snakes stopped winding up and down his arms and the road ahead became steady and clearer. He'd never liked the Stones much. A load of wankers, really, though you had to admit Jagger had a style of his own which no one could copy. But basically wankers like the rest of the current posers, like Morrison and Alice Cooper. It occurred to him he was wasting his time thinking about nothing but bands, but what else was there to think about? Anyway how else could you see your life? The mystical thing didn't mean much to him. Scientology was a load of crap. At any rate, he couldn't see anything in it. The guys running all that stuff seemed to be more hung-up than the people they were supposed to be helping. That was true of a lot of things. Most people who told you they wanted to help you were getting off on you in some way. He'd met pretty much every kind of freak by now. Sufis, Hare Krishnas, Jesus Freaks, Meditators, Processors, Divine Lighters. They could all talk better than him, but they all seemed to need more from him than they could give. You get into people when you were tripping. Acid had done a lot for him that way. He could suss out the hype-merchants so easily these days. And by that test Jimi couldn't be a fake. Jimi was straight. Fucked up now, possibly, but okay.

The road was long and white and then it became a big boulder. Mo couldn't tell if the boulder was real or not. He drove at it, then changed his mind, braking sharply. A red car behind him swerved and hooted as it went past him through the boulder which disappeared. Mo shook all over. He took out the Stones tape and changed it for the Grateful Dead's *American Beauty,* turned down low.

"You okay, man?" said Hendrix.

"Sure. Just a bit shakey." Mo started the Merc up.

"You want to stop and get some sleep."

"I'll see how I feel later."

It was sunset when Jimi said: "We seem to be heading south."

"Yeah," said Mo. "I need to get to London."

"You got to score?"

"Yeah."

"Maybe I'll come in with you this time."

"Yeah?"

"Maybe I won't."

CHAPTER SEVEN

By the time Mo had hitched to the nearest tube station and reached Ladbroke Grove he was totally wasted. The images were all inside his head now: pictures of Jimi from the first time he'd seen him on TV playing *Hey, Joe* (Mo had still been at school then), pictures of Jimi playing at Woodstock, at festivals and gigs all over the country. Jimi in big, feathered hats, bizarre multi-coloured shirts, several rings on each finger, playing that white Strat, flinging the guitar over his head, plucking the strings with his teeth, shoving it under his straddled legs, making it wail and moan and throb, doing more with a guitar then anyone had done before. Only Jimi could make a guitar come alive in that way, turning the machine into an organic creature, simultaneously a prick, a woman, a white horse, a sliding snake. Mo glanced at his arms, but they were still. The sun was beginning to set as he turned into Lancaster Road, driven more by a mixture of habit and momentum than any energy or sense of purpose. He had another image in his head now, of Jimi as a soul thief, taking the energy away from the audience. Instead of a martyr, Jimi became the vampire. Mo knew that the paranoia was really setting in and the sooner he got hold of some uppers the better. He couldn't blame Jimi for how he felt. He hadn't slept for two days. That was all it was. Jimi had given everything to the people in the audience, including his life. How many people in the audience had died for Jimi?

He crawled up the steps of the house in Lancaster Road and rang the third bell down. There was no answer. He was shaking badly. He held on to the concrete steps and tried to calm himself, but it got worse and he thought he was going to pass out.

The door behind him opened.

"Mo?"

It was Dave's chick, Jenny, wearing a purple brocade dress. Her hair was caked with wet henna.

"Mo? You all right?"

Mo swallowed and said: "Hullo, Jenny. Where's Dave?"

"He went down the Mountain Grill to get something to eat. About half an hour ago. Are you all right, Mo?"

"Tired. Dave got any uppers?"

"He had a lot of mandies in."

Mo accepted the news. "Can you let me have a couple of quids' worth?"

"You'd better ask him yourself, Mo. I don't know who he's promised them to."

Mo nodded and got up carefully.

"You want to come in and wait, Mo?" said Jenny.

Mo shook his head. "I'll go down the Mountain. See you later, Jenny."

"See you later, Mo. Take care, man."

Mo shuffled slowly up Lancaster Road and turned the corner into Portobello Road. He thought he saw the black and chrome Merc cross the top of the street. The buildings were all crowding in on him.

He saw them grinning at him, leering. He heard them talking about him. There were fuzz everywhere. A woman threw something at him. He kept going until he reached the Mountain Grill and stumbled through the door. The café was crowded with freaks but there was nobody there he knew. They all had evil, secretive expressions and they were whispering.

"You fuckers," he mumbled, but they pretended they weren't listening. He saw Dave.

"Dave? Dave, man!"

Dave looked up, grinning privately. "Hi, Mo. When did you get back to town?" He was dressed in new, clean denims with fresh patches on them. One of the patches said "Star Rider".

"Just got in." Mo leaned across the tables, careless of the intervening people, and whispered in Dave's ear. "I hear you got some mandies."

Dave's face became serious. "Sure. Now?"

Mo nodded.

Dave rose slowly and paid his bill to the dark, fat lady at the till. "Thanks, Maria."

Dave took Mo by the shoulder and led him out of the café. Mo wondered if Dave was about to finger him. He remembered that Dave had been suspected more than once.

Dave said softly as they went along. "How many d'you need, Mo?"

"How much are they?"

Dave said: "You can have them for ten p each."

"I'll have five quids' worth. A hundred, yeah?"

"Fifty."

They got back to Lancaster Road and Dave let himself in with two keys, a Yale and a mortise. They went up a dark, dangerous stairway. Dave's room was gloomy, thick with incense, with painted blinds covering the window. Jenny sat on a mattress in the corner listening to Ace on the stereo. She was knitting.

"Hi, Mo," she said. "So you found him."

Mo sat down on the mattress in the opposite corner. "How's it going, Jenny?" he said. He didn't like Dave, but he liked Jenny. He made a big effort to be polite. Dave was standing by a chest of drawers, dragging a box from under a pile of tasselled curtains. Mo looked past him and saw Jimi standing there. He was dressed in a hand-painted silk shirt with roses all over it. There was a jade talisman on a silver chain round his throat. He had the white Strat in his hands. His eyes were closed as he played it. Almost immediately Mo guessed he was looking at a poster.

Dave counted fifty mandies into an aspirin bottle. Mo reached into his jeans and found some money. He gave Dave a five pound note and Dave gave him the bottle. Mo opened the bottle and took out a lot of the pills, swallowing them fast. They didn't act right away, but he felt better for taking them. He got up.

"See you later, Dave."

"See you later, man," said Dave. "Maybe in Finch's tonight."

"Yeah."

CHAPTER EIGHT

Mo couldn't remember how the fight started. He'd been sitting quietly in a corner of the pub drinking his pint of bitter when that big fat fart who was always in there causing trouble decided to pick on him. He remembered getting up and punching the fat fart. There had been a lot of confusion then and he had somehow knocked the fat fart over the bar. Then a few people he knew pulled him away and took him back to a basement in Oxford Gardens where he listened to some music.

It was *Band of Gipsys* that woke him up. Listening to *Machine Gun* he realized suddenly that he didn't like it. He went to the pile of records and found other Hendrix albums. He played *Are You Experienced?*, the first album, and *Electric Ladyland*, and he liked them much better. Then he played *Band of Gipsys* again.

He looked round the dark room. Everyone seemed to be totally spaced out.

"He died at the right time," he said. "It was over for him, you know. He shouldn't have come back."

He felt in his pocket for his bottle of mandies. There didn't seem to be that many left. Maybe someone had ripped them off in the pub. He took a few more and reached for the bottle of wine on the table, washing them down. He put *Are You Experienced?* on the deck again and lay back. "That was really great," he said. He fell asleep. He shook a little bit. His breathing got deeper and deeper. When he started to vomit in his sleep nobody noticed. By that time everyone was right out of it. He choked quietly and then stopped.

CHAPTER NINE

About an hour later a black man came into the room. He was tall and elegant. He radiated energy. He wore a white silk shirt and white jeans. There were shiny patent leather boots on his feet. A chick started to get up as he came into the room. She looked bemused.

"Hi," said the newcomer. "I'm looking for Mo Beck. We ought to be going."

He peered at the sleeping bodies and then looked closer at one which lay a little apart from the others. There was vomit all over his face and all over his shirt. His skin was a ghastly, dirty green. The black man stepped across the others and knelt beside Mo, feeling his heart, taking his pulse.

The chick stared stupidly at him. "Is he all right?"

"He's O-D'd," the newcomer said quietly. "He's gone. D'you want to get a doctor or something, honey?"

"Oh, Jesus," she said.

The black man got up and walked to the door.

"Hey," she said. "You look just like Jimi Hendrix, you know that?"

"Sure."

"You can't be—you're not, are you? I mean, Jimi's dead."

Jimi shook his head and smiled his old smile. "Shit, lady. They can't kill Jimi." He laughed as he left.

The chick glanced down at the small, ruined body covered in its own vomit. She swayed a little, rubbing at her thighs. She frowned. Then she went as quickly as she could from the room, hampered by her long cotton dress, and into the street. It was nearly dawn and it was cold. The tall figure in the white suit and jeans didn't seem to notice the cold. It strode up to the big Mercedes camper parked near the end of the street.

The chick began to run after the black truck as it started up and rolled a little way before it had to stop on the red light at the Ladbroke Grove intersection.

"Wait," she shouted. "Jimi!"

But the camper was moving before she could reach it.

She saw it heading north towards Kilburn.

She wiped the clammy sweat from her face. She must be freaking. She hoped when she got back to the basement that there wouldn't really be a dead guy there.

She didn't need it.

In memory, among others,
of Smiling Mike and John the Bog

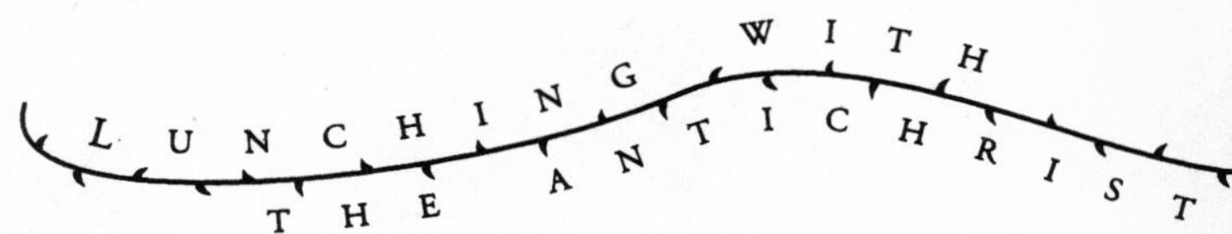
LUNCHING WITH
THE ANTICHRIST

LUNCHING WITH THE ANTICHRIST

Begg Mansions,
Sporting Club Square

The Editor,
Fulham & Hammersmith Telegraph,
Bishops Palace Avenue,
London W14

13th October 1992

Sir,

SPIRIT OF THE BLITZ

It is heartening to note, as our economy collapses perhaps for the last time, a return to the language and sentiments of mutual self-interest. London was never the kindest of English cities but of late her cold, self-referential greed has been a watchword around the world. Everything we value is threatened in the name of profit.

I say nothing original when I mourn the fact that it took the Blitz to make Londoners achieve a humanity and heroism they never thought to claim for themselves and which no one expected or demanded of them!

Could we not again aspire to achieve that spirit, without the threat of Hitler but with the same optimistic courage? Can we not, in what is surely an hour of need, marshall what is best in us and find new means of achieving that justice, equity and security for which we all long? The existing methods appear to create as many victims as they save.

Yours faithfully, Edwin Begg,
former vicar of St. Odhran's, Balham.

HEAR! HEAR! says the Telegraph. This week's Book Token to our Letter of the Week! Remember, your opinions are important to us and we want to see them! A £5.00 Book Token for the best!

ONE

My First Encounter With the Clapham Anti-Christ; His Visions & His Public Career; His Expulsion from the Church & Subsequent Notoriety; His Return To Society & Celebrity as a Sage; His Mysterious & Abrupt Departure Into Hermitage; His Skills in the Kitchen.

"SPIRIT OF THE BLITZ" (a sub-editor's caption) was the last public statement of the Clapham Antichrist.

Until I read the letter at a friend's I believed Edwin Begg dead some twenty years ago. The beloved TV eccentric had retired in the 1950s to live as a recluse in Sporting Club Square, West Kensington. I had known him intimately in the 60s and 70s and was shocked to learn he was still alive. I felt a conflicting mixture of emotions, including guilt. Why had I so readily accepted the hearsay of his death? I wrote to him at once. Unless he replied to the contrary I would visit him on the following Wednesday afternoon.

Lunching With the Antichrist

MICHAEL MOORCOCK

I had met Begg first in 1966 when as a young journalist I interviewed him for a series in the *Star* about London's picturesque obscurities. Then too I had contacted him after reading one of his letters to the *Telegraph*. The paper, still a substantial local voice, was his only source of news, delivered to him weekly. He refused to have a telephone and communicated mostly through the post.

I had hoped to do a few paragraphs on the Antichrist's career, check a couple of facts with him and obtain a short, preferably amusing, comment on our Fab Sixties. I was delighted when, with cheerful courtesy, Edwin Begg had agreed by return to my request. In a barely legible old-fashioned hand he invited me to lunch.

My story was mostly drafted before I set off to see him. Research had been easy. We had half a filing drawer on Edwin Begg's years of notoriety, first before the War then afterwards as a radio and early TV personality. He had lived in at least a dozen foreign cities. His arguments were discussed in every medium and he became a disputed symbol. Many articles about him were merely sensational, gloating over alleged black magic rites, sexual deviation, miracle-working, blasphemy and sorcery. There were the usual photographs and also drawings, some pretending to realism and others cruel cartoons: the Clapham Antichrist as a monster with blazing eyes and glittering fangs, architect of the doom to come. One showed Hitler, Stalin and Mussolini as his progeny.

The facts were pretty prosaic; in 1931 at the age of 24 Begg was vicar of St. Odhran's, Balham, a shabby North London living where few parishioners considered themselves respectable enough to visit a church and were darkly suspicious of those who did. The depression years had almost as many homeless and hungry people on the streets as today. Mosley was gathering a more militant flock than Jesus and those who opposed the Fascists looked to Oxford or the secular left for their moral leadership. Nonetheless the Reverend Begg conscientiously performed his duty, offering the uncertain comforts of his calling to his flock.

Then quite suddenly in 1933 the ordinary hard-working cleric became an urgent proselytiser, an orator. From his late Victorian pulpit he began preaching a shocking message urging Christians to act according to their principles and sacrifice their own material ambitions to the common good, to take a risk on God being right, as he put it. This Tolstoyan exhortation eventually received enough public attention to make his sermons one of London's most popular free attractions from Southwark to Putney, which of course brought him the attention of the famous Bermondsey barrackers, the disapproval of his establishment and the closer interest of the press.

The investigators the Church sent down heard a sermon touching mainly on the current state of the Spanish Republic, how anarchists often acted more like ideal Christians than the priests, how people seemed more willing to give their lives to the anarchists than to the cause of Christ. This was reported in *Reynolds News*, tipped off that the investigators would be there, as Begg's urging his congregation to support the coming Antichrist. The report was more or less approving. The disapproving church investigators, happy for a lead to follow, confirmed the reports. Overnight, the Reverend Edwin Begg, preaching his honest Christian message of brotherly love and equity under the law, became the Clapham Antichrist, Arch Enemy of British Decency, Proud Mocker of All Religion and Hitler's Right Hand, a creature to be driven from our midst.

In the course of a notoriously hasty hearing Edwin Begg was unfrocked, effectively by public demand. In his famous defence Begg confirmed the general opinion of his guilt by challenging the commission to strip itself naked and follow Christ, if they were indeed Christians! He made a disastrous joke: and if they were an example of modern Christians, he said, then after all he probably was the Antichrist!

Begg never returned to his vicarage. He went immediately to Sporting Club Square. Relatives took him in, eventually giving him his own three-roomed flat where it was rumoured he kept a harem of devil-worshipping harlots. The subsequent Siege of Sporting Club Square in which the *News of the World* provoked a riot causing one near-fatality and thousands of pounds worth of damage was overshadowed by the news of Hitler's massacre of his stormtroopers, the S.A. Goebbels' propaganda became more interesting and rather more in the line of an authentic harbinger of evil, and at last Edwin Begg was left in peace.

Usually attached to a circus or a fair and always billed as "Reverend" Begg, The Famous Clapham Antichrist! he began to travel the country with his message of universal love. After his first tours he was never a great draw since he disappointed audiences with urgent pleas for sanity and the common good and never rose to the jokes or demands for miracles, but at least he had discovered a way of making a living from his vocation. He spent short periods in prison and there were rumours of a woman in his life, someone he had mentioned early on, though not even the worst of the Sundays found evidence to suggest he was anything but confirmed in his chastity.

When the War came Edwin Begg distinguished himself in the ambulance service, was wounded and decorated. Then he again disappeared from public life. This was his first long period of seclusion in Begg Mansions until suddenly on 1 May, 1949, encouraged by his cousin Robert in BBC Talks, he gave at 9:45 pm on the Home Service the first of his Fireside Observer chats.

No longer the Old Testament boom of the pulpit or the sideshow, the Fireside Observer's voice was level, reassuring, humorous, a little sardonic sometimes when referring to authority. He reflected on our continuing hardships and what we might gain through them if we kept trying—what we might expect to see for our children. He offered my parents a vision of a wholesome future worth working for, worth making a few sacrifices for, and they loved him.

He seemed the moral spirit of the Festival of Britain, the best we hoped to become, everything that was decent about being British. An entire book was published proving him the object of a plot in 1934 by a Tory bishop, a Fascist sympathiser, and there were dozens of articles, newsreels and talks describing him as the victim of a vicious hoax or showing how Mosley had needed a scapegoat.

Begg snubbed the Church's willingness to review his case in the light of his new public approval and continued to broadcast the reassuring ironies which lightened our 1950s darkness and helped us create the golden years of the 1960s and 70s. He did not believe his dream to be illusory.

By 1950 he was on television, part of the *Thinker's Club* with Gilbert Harding and Professor Joad, which every week discussed an important contemporary issue. The programme received the accolade of being lampooned in *Radio Fun* as *The Stinker's Club* with Headwind Legg which happened to be one of my own childhood favourites. He appeared, an amiable sage, on panel games, quiz shows, programmes called *A Crisis of Faith* or *Turning Point* and at religious conferences eagerly displaying their tolerance by soliciting the opinion of a redeemed antichrist.

Suddenly, in 1955, Begg refused to renew all broadcasting contracts and retired from public life, first to travel and finally to settle back in Begg Mansions with his books and his journals. He never explained his decision and then the public lost interest. New men with brisker messages were bustling in to build utopia for us in our lifetime.

Contenting himself with a few letters mostly on parochial matters to the Hammersmith *Telegraph*, Edwin Begg lived undisturbed for a decade. His works of popular philosophy sold steadily until British fashion changed. Writing nothing after 1955, he encouraged his books to go out of print. He kept his disciples, of course, who sought his material in increasingly obscure places and wrote to him concerning his uncanny understanding of their deepest feelings, the ways in which he had dramatically changed their lives, and to whom, it was reported, he never replied.

The first Wednesday I took the 28 from Notting Hill Gate down North Star Road to Greyhound Gardens. I had brought my A-Z. I had never been to Sporting Club Square before and was baffled by the surrounding network of tiny twisting streets, none of which seemed to go in the same direction for more than a few blocks, the result of frenzied rival building work during the speculative 1880s when developers had failed to follow the plans agreed between themselves, the freeholder, the architect and the authorities. The consequent recession ensured that nothing was ever done to remedy the mess. Half-finished crescents and abrupt culs-de-sac, odd patches of wasteland, complicated rights of way involving narrow alleys, walls, gates and ancient pathways were interrupted, where bomb damage allowed, by the new council estates, totems of clean enlightenment geometry whose erection would automatically cause all surrounding social evils to wither away. I had not expected to find anything quite so depressing and began to feel sorry for Begg ending his days in such circumstances, but turning out of Margrave Passage I came suddenly upon a cluster of big unkempt oaks and cedars gathered about beautiful wrought-iron gates in the baroque oriental regency style of Old Cogges, that riot of unnatural ruin, the rural seat of the Beggs which William the Goth remodelled in 1798 to rival Strawberry Hill. They were miraculous in the early afternoon sun: the gates to paradise.

The square now has a preservation order and appears in international books of architecture as the finest example of its kind. Sir Hubert Begg, its architect, is mentioned in the same breath as Gaudi and Norman Shaw, which will give you some notion of his peculiar talent. Inspired by the fluid aesthetics of the *fin-de-siècle* he was loyal to his native brick and fired almost every fancy from Buckingham clay to give his vast array of disparate styles an inexplicable coherence. The tennis courts bear the motifs of some Mucha-influenced smith, their floral metalwork garlanded with living roses and honeysuckle from spring until autumn: even the benches are on record as one of the loveliest expressions of public *art nouveau.*

Until 1960 there had been a black chain across the Square's entrance and a porter on duty day and night. Residents' cars were never seen in the road but garaged in the little William Morris cottages originally designed as studios and running behind the eccentrically magnificent palaces, which had been Begg's Folly until they survived the Blitz to become part of our heritage. When I walked up to the gates in 1966 a few cars had appeared in the gravel road running around gardens enclosed by other leafy ironwork after Charles Rennie Mackintosh, and the Square had a bit of a shamefaced seedy appearance.

There were only a few uniformed porters on part-time duty by then and they too had a slightly hangdog air. The Square was weathering one of its periodic declines, having again failed to connect with South Kensington during a decade of prosperity. Only the bohemian middle classes were actually proud to live there, so the place had filled with actors, music hall performers, musicians, singers, writers, cheque-kiters and artists of every kind, together with journalists, designers and retired dance instructresses, hair-dressers and disappointed legatees muttering bitterly about any blood not their own, for the Square had taken refugees and immigrants. Others came to be near the tennis courts maintained by the SCS Club affiliated to nearby Queen's.

Several professionals had taken apartments in Wratislaw Villas, so the courts never went down and neither did the gardens which were preserved by an endowment from Gordon Begg, Lord Mauleverer, the botanist and explorer, whose elegant vivarium still pushed its flaking white girders and steamy glass above exotic shrubbery near the Mandrake Road entrance. Other examples of his botanical treasures, the rival of Holland's, flourished here and there about the Square and now feathery exotics mingled with the oaks and hawthorn of the original Saxon meadow.

Arriving in this unexpected tranquility on a warm September afternoon when the dramatic red sun gave vivid contrast to the terracotta, the deep greens of trees, lawns and shrubbery, I paused in astonished delight. Dreamily I continued around the Square in the direction shown me by the gatehouse porter. I was of a generation which enthused over pre-Raphaelite paint and made Beardsley its own again, who had bought the five shilling Mackintosh chairs and sixpenny Muchas and ten bob Lalique glass in Portobello Road to decorate Liberty-oriental pads whose fragrant patchouli never disguised the pungent dope. They were the best examples we could find in this world to remind us of what we had seen on our acid voyages.

To my father's generation the Square would be unspeakably old-fashioned, redolent of the worst suburban pretension, but I had come upon a gorgeous secret. I understood why so few people mentioned it, how almost everyone was either enchanted or repelled. My contemporaries, who thought "Georgian" the absolute height of excellence and imposed their stern developments upon Kensington's levelled memory, found Sporting Club Square hideously "Victorian"—a gigantic, grubby whatnot. Others dreamed of the day when they would have the power to be free of Sporting Club Square, the power to raze her and raise their fake Le Corbusier mile-high concrete in triumph above the West London brick.

I did not know, as I made my way past great mansions of Caligari Tudor and Kremlin De Mille, that I was privileged to find the Square in the final years of her glory. In those days I enjoyed a wonderful innocence and could no more visualise this lovely old place changing for the worse than I could imagine the destruction of Dubrovnik.

Lunching With the Antichrist

MICHAEL MOORCOCK

Obscured, sometimes, by her trees, the mansion apartments of Sporting Club Square revealed a thousand surprises. I was in danger of being late as I stared at Rossettian gargoyles and Blakean caryatids, copings, gables, corbels of every possible stamp yet all bearing the distinctive style of their time. I was filled with an obscure sense of epiphany.

In 1886, asymmetrical Begg Mansions was the boldest expression of modernism, built by the architect for his own family use, for his offices and studios, his living quarters, a suite to entertain clients, and to display his designs, accommodation for his draughts- and craftspeople whose studios in attics and basements produced the prototype glass, metal, furniture and fabrics which nowadays form the basis of the V&A's extraordinary collection. By the 1920s after Hubert Begg's death the Square became unfashionable. Lady Begg moved to Holland Park and Begg Mansions filled up with the poorer Beggs who paid only the communal fee for general upkeep and agreed to maintain their own flats in good condition. Their acknowledged patron was old Squire Begg, who had the penthouse. By 1966 the building was a labyrinth of oddly twisting corridors and stairways, unexpected landings reached by two old oak and copper cage elevators served by their own generator, which worked on an eccentric system devised by the architect and was always going wrong. Later I learned that it was more prudent to walk the six flights to Edwin Begg's rooms but on that first visit I got into the lift, pressed the stud for the sixth floor and was taken up without incident in a shower of sparks and rattling brass to the ill-lit landing where the Antichrist himself awaited me.

I recognised him of course but was surprised that he seemed healthier than I had expected. He was a little plumper and his bone-white hair was cropped in a self-administered pudding-basin cut. He was clean shaven, pink and bright as a mouse, with startling blue eyes, a firm rather feminine mouth and the long sharp nose of his mother's Lowland Presbyterian forefathers. His high voice had an old-fashioned Edwardian elegance and was habitually rather measured. He reminded me of a Wildean *grande-dame*, tiny but imposing. I was dressed like most of my Ladbroke Grove peers and he seemed pleased by my appearance, offering me his delicate hand, introducing himself and muttering about my good luck with the lift. He had agreed to this interview, he said, because he'd been feeling unusually optimistic after playing the new Beatles album. We shared our enthusiasm.

He guided me back through those almost organic passages until we approached his flat and a smell so heady, so delicious that I did not at first identify it as food. His front door let directly onto his study which led to a sitting room and bedroom. Only the dining room seemed unchanged since 1900 and still had the original Voysey wallpaper and furniture, a Henry dresser and Benson copperware. Like many reclusive people he enjoyed talking. As he continued to cook he sat me on a sturdy Wilson stool with a glass of wine and asked me about my career, showing keen interest in my answers.

"I hope you don't mind home cooking," he said. "It's a habit I cultivated when I lived on the road. Is there anything you find disagreeable to eat?"

I would have eaten strychnine if it had tasted as that first meal tasted. We had mysterious sauces whose nuances I can still recall, wines of exquisite delicacy, a dessert which contained an entire orchestra of flavours, all prepared in his tiny perfect 1920s "modern" kitchenette to one side of the dining room.

After we had eaten he suggested we take our coffee into the bedroom to sit in big wicker chairs and enjoy another wonderful revelation. He drew the curtains back from his great bay window to reveal over two miles of almost unbroken landscape all the way to the river with the spires and roofs of Old Putney beyond. In the far distance was a familiar London skyline but immediately before us were the Square's half-wild communal gardens and cottage garages, then the ivy-covered walls of St. Mary's Convent, the Convent School sports field and that great forest of shrubs, trees and memorial sculptures, the West London Necropolis, whose Victorian angels raised hopeful swords against the ever-changing sky. Beyond the cemetery was the steeple of St. Swithold's and her churchyard, then a nurtured patchwork of allotments, some old alms cottages and finally the sturdy topiary of the Bishop's Gardens surrounding a distant palace whose Tudor dignity did much to inspire Hubert Begg. The formal hedges marched all the way to the bird sanctuary on a broad, marshy curve where the Thames approached Hammersmith Bridge, a medieval fantasy.

It was the pastoral and monumental in perfect harmony which some cities spontaneously create. Edwin Begg said the landscape was an unfailing inspiration. He could dream of Roman galleys beating up the river cautiously alert for Celtic war-parties or Vikings striking at the Bishop's Palace leaving flames and murder behind. He liked to think of other more contemplative eyes looking on a landscape scarcely changed in centuries. "Hogarth, Turner and Whistler amongst them. Wheldrake, writing *Harry Wharton*, looked out from this site when staying at the Sporting Club Tavern and earlier Augusta Begg conceived the whole of *The Bravo of Bohemia* and most of *Yamboo; or, The North American Slave* while seated more or less where I am now! Before he went off to become an orientalist and London's leading painter of discrete seraglios James Lewis Porter painted several large landscapes which show market gardens where the allotments are, a few more cottages, but not much else has changed. I can walk downstairs, out of the back door, through that gate, cross the convent field into the graveyard, take the path through the church down to the allotments all the way to the Bishop's Gardens and be at the bird sanctuary within half-an-hour, even cross the bridge into Putney and the Heath if I feel like it and hardly see a house, a car or another human being!" He would always stop for a bun, he said, at the old

Palace Tea Rooms and usually strolled back via Margrave Avenue's interesting junkyards. Mrs. White, who kept the best used bookshop there, told me he came in at least twice a week.

He loved to wake up before dawn with his curtains drawn open and watch the sun gradually reveal familiar sights. "No small miracle, these days, dear! I'm always afraid that one morning it won't be there." At the time I thought this no more than a mildly philosophical remark.

For me he still had the aura of a mythic figure from my childhood, someone my parents had revered. I was prepared to dislike him but was immediately charmed by his gentle eccentricity, his rather loud plaid shirts and corduroys, his amiable vagueness. The quality of the lunch alone would have convinced me of his virtue!

I was of the 1960s, typically idealistic and opinionated and probably pretty obnoxious to him but he saw something he liked about me and I fell in love with him. He was my ideal father.

I returned home to rewrite my piece. A figure of enormous wisdom, he offered practical common sense, I said, in a world ruled by the abstract sophistries and empty reassurances heralding the new spirit of competition into British society. It was the only piece of mine the *Star* never used, but on that first afternoon Edwin Begg invited me back for lunch and on almost every Wednesday for the next eight years, even after I married, I would take the 28 from the Odeon, Westbourne Grove to Greyhound Gardens and walk through alleys of stained concrete, past shabby red terraces and doorways stinking of rot until I turned that corner and stood again before the magnificent gates of Sporting Club Square.

My friend kept his curiosity about me and I remained flattered by his interest. He was always fascinating company, whether expanding on some moral theme or telling a funny story. One of his closest chums had been Harry Lupino Begg, the music hall star, and he had also known Al Bowlly. He was a superb and infectious mimic and could reproduce Lupino's patter by heart, making it as topical and fresh as the moment. His imitation of Bowlly singing "Buddy, Can You Spare a Dime" was uncanny. When carried away by some amusing story or conceit his voice would rise and fall in rapid and entertaining profusion, sometimes taking on a birdlike quality difficult to follow. In the main however he spoke with the deliberate air of one who respected the effect of words upon the world.

By his own admission the Clapham Antichrist was not a great original thinker but he spoke from original experience. He helped me look again at the roots of my beliefs. Through him I came to understand the innocent intellectual excitement of the years before political experiments turned one by one into tyrannical orthodoxies. He loaned me my first Kropotkin, the touching *Memoirs of an Anarchist*, and helped me understand the difference between moral outrage and social effect. He loved works of popular intellectualism. He was as great an enthusiast for Huxley's *The Perennial Philosophy* as he was for Winwood Reade's boisterously secular *Martyrdom of Man*. He introduced me to the interesting late work of H.G. Wells and to Elizabeth Bowen. He led me to an enjoyment of Jane Austen I had never known. He infected me with his enthusiasm for the more obscure Victorians who remained part of his own living library and he was generous with his books. But, no matter how magical our afternoons, he insisted I must always be gone before the BBC broadcast Choral Evensong. Only in the dead of winter did I ever leave Sporting Club Square in darkness.

Naturally I was curious to know why he had retired so abruptly from public life. Had he told the church of his visions? Why had he felt such an urgent need to preach? To risk so much public disapproval? Eventually I asked him how badly it had hurt him to be branded as the premier agent of the Great Antagonist, the yapping dog as it were at the heels of the Son of the Morning. He said he had retreated from the insults before they had grown unbearable. "But it wasn't difficult to snub people who asked you questions like 'Tell me, Mr. Begg, what does human blood taste like?' Besides, I had my Rose to sustain me, my vision..."

I hoped he would expand on this but he only chuckled over some association he had made with an obscure temptation of St. Anthony and then asked me if I had been to see his cousin Orlando Begg's *Flaming Venus,* now on permanent display at the Tate.

Though I was soon addicted to his company, I always saw him on the same day and time every week. As he grew more comfortable with me he recounted the history of his family and Sporting Club Square. He spoke of his experiences as a young curate, as a circus entertainer, as a television personality, and he always cooked. This was, he said, the one time he indulged his gourmet instincts. In the summer we would stroll in the gardens or look at the tennis matches. Sitting on benches we would watch the birds or the children playing. When I asked him questions about his own life his answers became fuller, though never completely unguarded.

It was easy to see how in his determined naïveté he was once in such frequent conflict with authority.

"I remember saying, my dear, to the magistrate—Who does not admire the free-running, intelligent fox? And few, no matter how inconvenienced, begrudge him his prey which is won by daring raiding and quick wits, risking all. A bandit, your honour, one can admire and prepare against. There is even a stirring or two of romance for the brigand chief. But once the brigand becomes a baron that's where the balance goes wrong, eh, your honour? It gets unfair, I said to him. Our sympathies recognise these differences so why can't our laws? Our courts make us performers in pieces of simplistic fiction! Why do we continue to waste so much time? The magistrate said he found my last remark amusing and gave me the maximum sentence."

Part of Edwin Begg's authority came from his vivacity. As he sat across from me at the table, putting little pieces of chicken into his mouth, pausing to enjoy them, then launching off onto a quite different subject, he seemed determined to relish every experience, every moment. His manner offered a clue to his past. Could he be so entertaining because he might otherwise have to confront an unpleasant truth? Anyone raised in a post-Freudian world could make that guess. But it was not necessarily correct.

Sometimes his bright eyes would dart away to a picture or glance through a window and I learned to interpret this fleeting expression as one of pain or sadness. He admitted readily that he had retreated into his inner life, feeling he had failed in both his public and private missions. I frequently reassured him of his value, the esteem in which he was still held, but he was unconvinced.

"Life isn't a matter of linear consequences," he said. "We only try to make it look like that. Our job is not to force grids upon the world but to achieve harmony with nature."

At that time in my life such phrases made me reach for my hat, if not my revolver, but because I loved him so much I tried to understand what he meant. He believed that in our terror we imposed perverse linearity upon a naturally turbulent universe, that our perceptions of time were at fault since we saw the swirling cosmos as still or slow-moving just as a gnat doubtless sees us. He thought that those who overcame their brute terror of the truth soon attained the state of the angels.

The Clapham Antichrist was disappointed that I was not more sympathetic to the mystical aspects of the alternative society but because of my familiarity with its ideas was glad to have me for a devil's advocate. I was looking for a fast road to utopia and he had almost given up finding any road at all. Our solutions were wrong because our analysis was wrong, he said. We needed to rethink our fundamental principles and find better means of applying them. I argued that this would take too long. Social problems required urgent action. His attitude was an excuse for inaction. In the right hands there was nothing wrong with the existing tools.

"And what are the right hands, dear?" he asked. "Who makes the rules? Who keeps them, my dear?" He ran his thin fingers through hair which became a milky halo around his earnest face. "And how is it possible to make them and keep them when our logic insists on such oppressive linearity? We took opium into China and bled them of their silver. Now they send heroin to us to lay hands upon our currency! Am I the only one enjoying the irony? The Indians are reclaiming the Southwestern United States in a massive migration back into the old French and Spanish lands. The world is never still, is it, my dear?"

His alert features were full of tiny signals, humorous and anxious, enquiring and defiant, as he expanded on his philosophy one autumn afternoon. We strolled around the outer path enjoying the late roses and early chrysanthemums forming an archway roofed with fading honeysuckle. He wore his green raglan, his yellow scarf, his hideous turf accountant's trilby, and gestured with the blackthorn he always carried but hardly used. "The world is never still and yet we continue to live as if turbulence were not the natural order of things. We have no more attained our ultimate state than has our own star! We have scarcely glimpsed any more of the multiverse than a toad under a stone! We are part of the turbulence and it is in turbulence we thrive. Once that's understood, my dear, the rest is surely easy? Brute warfare is our crudest expression of natural turbulence, our least productive. What's the finest? Surely there's no evil in aspiring to be our best? What do we gain by tolerating or even justifying the worst?"

I sat down on the bench looking the length of a bower whose pale golds and browns were given a tawny burnish by the sun. Beyond the hedges was the sound of a tennis game. "And those were the ideas which so offended the Church?" I asked.

He chuckled, his face sharp with self-mockery. "Not really. They had certain grounds I suppose. I don't know. I merely suggested to my congregation after the newspapers had begun the debate, that perhaps only through Chaos and Anarchy could the Millennium be achieved. There was after all certain clues to that effect in the Bible. I scarcely think I'm to blame if this was interpreted as calling for bloody revolution, or heralding Armageddon and the Age of the Antichrist!"

I was diplomatic. "Perhaps you made the mistake of overestimating your audiences?"

Smiling he turned where he sat to offer me a reproving eye. "I did not overestimate them, my dear. They underestimated themselves. They didn't appreciate that I was trying to help them become one with the angels. I have experienced such miracles, my dear! Such wonderful visions!"

And then quite suddenly he had risen and taken me by my arm to the Duke's Elm, the ancient tree which marked the border of the larger square in what was really a cruciform. Beyond the elm were lawns and well-stocked beds of the cross's western bar laid out exactly as Begg had planned. Various residents had brought their deckchairs here to enjoy the last of the summer. There was a leisurely good-humoured holiday air to the day. It was then, quite casually and careless of passers-by, that the Clapham Antichrist described to me the vision which converted him from a mild-mannered Anglican cleric into a national myth.

"It was on a similar evening to this in 1933. Hitler had just taken power. I was staying with my Aunt Constance Cunningham, the actress, who had a flat in D'Yss Mansions and refused to associate with the other Beggs. I had come out here for a stroll to smoke my pipe and think over a few ideas for the next Sunday's sermon which I would deliver, my dear, to a congregation consisting mostly of the miserably senile and the irredeemably small-minded who came to church primarily as a signal to neighbours they believed beneath them…

"It was a bloody miserable prospect. I have since played better audiences on a wet Thursday night in a ploughed field outside Leeds. No matter what happened to me I never regretted leaving those dour ungiving faces behind. I did my best. My sermons were intended to discover the smallest flame of charity and aspiration burning in their tight little chests. I say all this in sad retrospect. At the time I was wrestling with my refusal to recognise certain truths and find a faith not threatened by them.

"I really was doing my best, my dear." He sighed and looked upward through the lattice of branches at the jackdaw nests just visible amongst the fading leaves. "I was quite agitated about my failure to discover a theme appropriate to their lives. I wouldn't give in to temptation and concentrate on the few decent parishioners at the expense of the rest." He turned to look across the lawns at the romantic rococo splendour of Moreau Mansions. "It was a misty evening in the Square with the sun setting through those big trees over there, a hint of pale gold in the haze and bold comforting shadows on the grass. I stood here, my dear, by the Duke's Elm. There was nobody else around. My vision stepped forward, out of the mist, and smiled at me.

"At first I thought that in my tiredness I was hallucinating. I'd been trained to doubt any ecstatic experience. The scent of roses was intense, like a drug! Could this be Carterton's ghost said to haunt the spot where he fell to his death, fighting a duel in the branches after a drunken night at Begg's? But this was no young duke. The woman was about my own height, with graceful beauty and the air of peace I associated with the Virgin. My unconventional madonna stood in a mannish confident way, a hand on her hip, clearly amused by me. She appeared to have emerged from the earth or from the tree. Shadows of bark and leaves still clung to her. There was something plant-like about the set of her limbs, the subtle colours of her flesh, as if a rose had become human and yet remained thoroughly a rose. I was rather frightened at first, my dear.

"I'd grown up with an Anglicanism permitting hardly a hint of the Pit, so I didn't perceive her as a temptress. I was thoroughly aware of her sexuality and in no way threatened by it or by her vitality. After a moment the fear dissipated, then after a few minutes she vanished and I was left with what I could only describe as her inspiration which led me to write my first real sermon that evening and present it on the following Sunday."

"She gave you a message?" I thought of Jeanne D'Arc.

"Oh, no. Our exchange was wordless on that occasion."

"And you spoke of her in church?"

"Never. That would have been a sort of betrayal. No, I based my message simply on the emotion she had aroused in me. A vision of Christ might have done the same. I don't know."

"So it was a Christian message? Not anti-Christian?"

"Not anti-religious, at any rate. Perhaps, as the bishop suggested, a little pagan."

"What brought you so much attention?"

"In the church that Sunday were two young chaps escorting their recently widowed aunt, Mrs. Nye. They told their friends about me. To my delight when I gave my second sermon I found myself with a very receptive congregation. I thanked God for the miracle. It seemed nothing else, my dear. You can't imagine the joy of it! For any chap in my position. I'd received a gift of divine communication, perhaps a small one, but it seemed pretty authentic. And the people began to pack St. Odhran's. We had money for repairs. They seemed so willing suddenly to give themselves to their faith!"

I was mildly disappointed. This Rose did not seem much of a vision. Under the influence of drugs or when overtired I had experienced hallucinations quite as elaborate and inspiring. I asked him if he had seen her again.

"Oh, yes. Of course. Many times. In the end we fell in love. She taught me so much. Later there was a child."

He stood up, adjusted his overcoat and scarf and gave his stick a little flourish. He pointed out how the light fell through the parade of black gnarled maples leading to the tennis courts. "An army of old giants ready to march," he said. "But their roots won't let them."

The next Wednesday when I came to lunch he said no more about his vision.

TWO

A Brief History of the Begg Family & of Sporting Club Square

In the course of my first four hundred lunches with the Clapham Antichrist I never did discover why he abandoned his career but I learned a great deal about the Begg family, its origins, its connections and its property, especially the Square. I became something of an expert and planned a monograph until the recent publication of two excellent Hubert Begg books made my work only useful as an appendix to real scholarship.

Today the Square, on several tourist itineraries, has lost most traces of its old unselfconscious integrity. Only Begg Mansions remains gated and fenced from casual view, a defiantly private museum of human curiosities. The rest of the Square has been encouraged to maximise its profitability. Bakunin Villas is now the Hotel Romanoff. Ralph Lauren for some time sponsored D'Yss Mansions as a fashion gallery. Beardsley Villas is let as company flats to United Foods, while the council (which invested heavily in BBIC) took another building, the Moorish fantasy of Flecker Mansions, as offices. There is still some talk of an international company "theme-parking" Sporting Club Square, running commercial tennis matches and linking it to a television soap. Following the financial scandals involving Begg Belgravia International and its associate companies, the Residents' Association has had some recent success in reversing this progress.

When I visited Edwin Begg in 1992, he welcomed me as if our routine had never been broken. He mourned his home's decline into a mere fashion, an exploitable commodity instead of a respected eccentricity, and felt it had gone the way of the Chateau Pantin or Derry & Toms famous Roof Garden, with every feature displayed as an emphatic curiosity, a sensation, a mode, and all her old charm a wistful memory. He had early on warned them about these likely consequences of his nephew's eager speculations. "Barbican wasn't the first to discover what you could do in a boom economy with a lick of paint, but I thought his soiling of his own nest a remote chance, not one of his first moves! The plans of such people are generally far advanced before they achieve power. When they strike you are almost always taken unawares, aren't you, dear? What cold, patient dreams they must have."

He derived no satisfaction from Barbican Begg's somewhat ignoble ruin but felt deep sympathy for his fellow residents hopelessly trying to recover their stolen past.

"It's too late for us now and soon it won't matter much, but it's hard to imagine the kind of appetite which feeds upon souls like locusts on corn. We might yet drive the locust from our field, my dear, but he has already eaten his fill. He has taken what we cannot replace."

Sometimes he was a little difficult to follow and his similes grew increasingly bucolic.

"The world's changing physically, dear. Can't you feel it?" His eyes were as bright a blue and clear as always, his pink cheeks a little more drawn, his white halo thinner, but he still pecked at the middle-distance when he got excited, as if he could tear the truth from the air with his nose. He was clearly delighted that we had resumed our meetings. He apologised that the snacks were things he could make and microwave. They were still delicious. On our first meeting I was close to tears, wondering why on earth I had simply assumed him dead and deprived myself of his company for so long. He suggested a stroll if I could stand it.

I admitted that the Square was not improving. I had been appalled at the gaudy golds and purples of the Hotel Romanoff. It was, he said, currently in receivership, and he shrugged. "What is it, my dear, which allows us to become the victims of such villains, time after time! Time after time they take what is best in us and turn it to our disadvantage. It's like being a conspirator in one's own rape."

We had come up to the Duke's Elm again in the winter twilight and he spoke fondly of familiar ancestors.

Cornelius van Beek, a Dutch cousin of the Saxon von Beks, had settled in London in 1689, shortly after William and Mary. For many Europeans in those days England was a haven of relative enlightenment. A daring merchant banker, van Beek financed exploratory trading expeditions, accompanying several of them himself, and amassed the honourable fortune enabling him to retire at sixty to Cogges Hall, Sussex. Amongst his properties when he died were the North Star Farm and tavern, west of Kensington, bought on the mistaken assumption that the area was growing more respectable and where he had at one time planned to build a house. This notorious stretch of heath was left to van Beek's nephew, George Arthur Begg who had anglicised his name upon marriage to Harriet Vernon, his second cousin, in 1738. Their only surviving grandson was Robert Vernon Begg, famous as Dandy Bob Begg and ennobled under the Prince Regent.

As financially impecunious as his patron, Dandy Bob raised money from co-members of the Hellfire, took over the old tavern at North Star Farm, increased its size and magnificence, entertained the picaro captains so they would go elsewhere for their prizes, ran bare-knuckle fights, bear-baitings and other brutal spectacles, and founded the most notorious sporting establishment of its day. Fortunes were commonly lost and won at Begg's; suicides, scandals and duels no rarity. A dozen of our oldest families spilled their blood in the meadow beneath the black elm, and perhaps a score of men and women drowned in the brook now covered and serving as a modern sewer.

Begg's Sporting Club grew so infamous, the activities of its members and their concubines such a public outrage, that when the next William ascended, Begg rapidly declined. By Victoria's crowning the great dandy whom all had courted had become a souse married into the Wadhams for their money, got his wife Charlotte pregnant with male twins and died, whereupon she somewhat boldly married his nephew Captain Russell Begg and had three more children before he died a hero and a colonel in the Crimea. The twins were Ernest Sumara and Louis Palmate Begg, her two girls were Adriana Circe and Juliana Aphrodite and her youngest boy, her favourite child, was Hubert Alhambra born on January 18th 1855 after his father's fatal fall at Balaclava.

A youthful disciple of Eastlake, by the late 1870s Hubert Begg was a practicing architect whose largest single commission was Castle Bothwell on the shores of Loch Ness (his sister had married James Bothwell) which became a victim of the Glasgow blitz. "But it was little more than a bit of quasi-Eastlake and no rival for instance to the V&A," Edwin Begg had told me. He did not share my admiration for his great-uncle's achievement. "Quite frankly, his best work was always his furniture." He was proud of his complete bedroom suite in Begg's rather spare late style but he did not delight in living in "an art nouveau wedding cake". He claimed the Square's buildings cost up to ten times as much to clean as Oakwood Mansions, for instance, at the western end of Kensington High Street. "Because of the crannies and fancy mouldings, those flowing fauns and smirking sylphs the late Victorians found so deliciously sexy. Dust traps all. It's certainly unique, my dear, but so was Quasimodo."

Lunching With the Antichrist

MICHAEL MOORCOCK

~

Hubert Begg never struggled for a living. He had married the beautiful Carinthia Hughes, an American heiress, during his two years in Baltimore and it was she who suggested he use family land for his own creation, tearing down that ramshackle old firetrap, The Sporting Club Tavern, which together with a smallholding was rented to a family called Foulsham whom Begg generously resettled on prime land, complete with their children, their cow, their pig and various other domestic animals, near Old Cogges.

The North Star land was cleared. North Star Square was named but lasted briefly as that. It was designed as a true square with four other smaller squares around it to form a sturdy box cross, thus allowing a more flexible way of arranging the buildings, ensuring residents plenty of light, good views and more tennis. Originally there were plans for seven tennis courts. By the 1880s tennis was a social madness rather than a vogue and everybody was playing. Nearby Queens Club was founded in Begg's shadow. Begg's plans were altogether more magnificent and soon the projected settlement blossomed into Sporting Club Square. The name had a slightly raffish, romantic reference and attracted the more daring young people, the financiers who still saw themselves as athletic privateers and who were already patrons to an artist or two as a matter of form.

Clients were encouraged to commission favourite styles for Begg to adapt. He had already turned his back on earlier influences, so Gothic did not predominate, but was well represented in Lohengrin Villas which was almost an homage to Eastlake, commissioned by the Church to house retired clergy who felt comfortable with its soaring arches and mighty buttresses. Encouraged by the enthusiasm for his scheme, the architect was able to indulge every fantasy, rather in the manner of a precocious Elgar offering adaptations of what Greaves called, in *The British Architect*, "Mediterranean, Oriental, Historical and Modern styles representing the quintessence of contemporary taste." But there were some who even then found it fussy and decadent. When the Queen praised it as an example to the world Begg was knighted. Lady Carinthia, who survived him by many years, always credited herself as the Square's real procreator and it must be said it was she who nudged her husband away from the past to embrace a more plastic future.

Work on Sporting Club Square began in 1885 but was not entirely completed until 1901. The slump of the 1890s destroyed the aspirations of the rising bourgeoisie, who were to have been the likely renters; Gibbs and Flew had bankrupted themselves building the Olympia Bridge, and nobody who still had money felt secure enough to cross into the new suburbs. Their dreams of elevation now frustrated, the failed and dispossessed took their new bitter poverty with them into the depths of a North Star development doomed never to rise and to become almost at once a watchword for social decrepitude, populated by loafers, psychopaths, unstable landladies, exploited seamstresses, drunkards, forgers, beaten wives, braggarts, embezzlers, rat-faced children, petty officials and prostitutes who had grown accustomed to the easy prosperity of the previous decade and were now deeply resentful of anyone more fortunate. They swiftly turned the district into everything it remained until the next tide of prosperity lifted it for a while, only to let it fall back almost in relief as another generation lost its hold upon life's ambitions. The terraces were occupied by casual labourers and petty thieves while the impoverished petite bourgeoisie sought the mews and parades. North Star became a synonym for wretchedness and miserable criminality and was usually avoided even by the police.

By 1935 the area was a warren to rival Notting Dale, but Sporting Club Square, the adjoining St. Mary's Convent and the churchyard, retained a rather dreamy, innocent air, untouched by the prevailing mood. Indeed locals almost revered and protected the

Square's tranquility as if it were the only thing they had ever held holy and were proud of it. During the last war the Square was untouched by incendiaries roaring all around, but some of the flats were already abandoned and then taken over by the government to house mostly Jewish political exiles and these added to the cosmopolitan atmosphere. For years a Polish delicatessen stood on the corner of North Star Road; it was possible to buy all kinds of kosher food at Mrs. Green's grocery, Mandrake Terrace, and the Foulsham Road French patisserie remained popular until 1980 when Madame Stejns retired. According to Edwin Begg, the war and the years of austerity were their best, with a marvellous spirit of cooperation everywhere. During the war and until 1954 open air concerts were regularly performed by local musicians and an excellent theatrical group was eventually absorbed into the Lyric until that was rationalised. A song, *The Rose of Sporting Club Square*, was popular in the 1930s and the musical play it was written for was the basis of a Hollywood musical in 1940. The David Glazier Ensemble, perhaps the most innovative modern dance troupe of its day, occupied all the lower flats in Le Gallienne Chambers.

Edwin Begg was not the only resident to become famous with the general public. Wheldrake's association with the old tavern, where he spent two years of exile, is well known. Audrey Vernon lived most of her short life in Dowson Mansions. Her lover, Warwick Harden, took a flat in Ibsen Studios next door and had a door built directly through to her bedroom. John Angus Gilchrist the mass murderer lived here but dispatched his nearest victim three miles away in Shepherd's Bush. Others associated with the Square, sometimes briefly, included Pett Ridge, George Robey, Gustav Klimt, Rebecca West, Constance Cummings, Jessie Matthews, Sonny Hale, Jack Parker, Gerald Kersh, Laura Riding, Joseph Kiss, John Lodwick, Edith Sitwell, Lord George Creech, Angela Thirkell, G.K. Chesterton, Max Miller, Sir Compton Mackenzie, Margery Allingham, Ralph Richardson,

Eudora Welty, Donald Peers, Max Wall, Dame Fay Westbrook, Graham Greene, Eduardo Paolozzi, Gore Vidal, Bill Butler, Jimi Hendrix, Jack Trevor Story, Laura Ashley, Mario Amayo, Angela Carter, Simon Russell Beale, Ian Dury, Jonathan Carroll and a variety of sports and media personalities. As its preserves were stripped, repackaged and sold off during the feeding frenzy of the 1980s only the most stubborn residents refused to be driven from the little holdings they had once believed their birthright, but it was not until Edwin Begg led me back to his bedroom and raised the newly-installed blind that I understood the full effect of his nephew's speculations. "We do not rest, do we," he said, "from mortal toil? But I'm not sure this is my idea of the new Jerusalem. What do you think, dear?"

They had taken his view, all that harmony. I was consumed with a sense of unspeakable outrage! They had turned that beautiful landscape into a muddy wasteland in which it seemed some monstrous, petulant child had scattered at random its filthy Tonka trucks and Corgi cranes, Portakabins, bulldozers in crazed abandon, then in tantrum stepped on everything. That perfect balance was destroyed and the tranquility of Sporting Club Square was now forever under siege. The convent was gone, as well as the church.

"I read in the *Telegraph* that it required the passage of two private member's bills, the defiance of several preservation orders, the bribery of officials in thirteen different government departments and the blackmailing of a cabinet minister just to annex a third of the cemetery and knock down the chapel and almshouses," Begg said.

Meanwhile the small fry had looted the cemetery of its saleable masonry. Every monument had been chiselled. The severed heads of the angels were already being sold in the antique boutiques of Mayfair and St. Germaine-des-Prés. Disappointed in their share of this loot, others had daubed swastikas and obscenities on the remaining stones.

"It's private building land now," said Begg. "They have dogs and fences. They bulldozed St. Swithold's. You can't get to the Necropolis, let alone the river. Still, this is probably better than what they were going to build."

The activities of Barbican Begg and his associates, whose enterprises claimed more victims than Maxwell, have been discussed everywhere, but one of the consequences of BBIC's speculations was that bleak no-man's-land standing in place of Edwin Begg's familiar view. The legal problems of leases sold to and by at least nine separate companies means that while no further development has added to the Square's decline, attempts to redress the damage and activate the Council's preservation orders which they ignored, have failed through lack of funds. The project, begun in the name of freedom and civic high-mindedness, always a mark of the scoundrel, remains a symbol and a monument to the asset-stripped 80s. As yet only Frank Cornelius, Begg's close associate, has paid any satisfactory price for ruining so many lives.

"Barbican was born for that age." Edwin Begg drew down the blind against his ruined prospect and sat on his bed, his frail body scarcely denting the great Belgian pillows at his back. "Like a fly born to a dungheap. He could not help himself, my dear. It was his instinct to do what he did. Why are we always surprised by his kind?"

He had grown weak but eagerly asked if I would return the following Wednesday when he would tell me more about his visions and their effect upon his life. I promised to bring the ingredients of a meal. I would cook lunch. He was touched and amused by this. He thought the idea great fun.

I told him to stay where he was. It was easy to let myself out.

"You know," he called as I was leaving, "there's a legend in our family. How we protect the Grail which will one day bring a reconciliation between God and Lucifer. I have no Grail to pass on to you but I think I have its secret."

THREE

*Astonishing Revelations of the Clapham Antichrist;
Claims Involvement in the Creation of a New Messiah;
His Visions of Paradise & Surrendering His Soul for Knowledge;
Further Description of the Sporting Club Square Madonna;
Final Days of the Antichrist; His Appearance In Death.*

"Perhaps the crowning irony," said the Clapham Antichrist of his unfrocking, "was how devoted a Christian I was then! I argued that we shouldn't wait for God or heroes but seek our solutions at the domestic level. Naturally, it would mean empowering everyone, because only a thoroughly enfranchised democracy ever makes the best of its people. Oh, well, you know the sort of thing. The universal ideal that we all agree on and never seem to achieve. I merely suggested we take a hard look at the systems we used! They were quite evidently faulty! Not an especially revolutionary notion! But it met with considerable antagonism as you know. Politics seems to be a war of labels, one slapped on top of another until any glimmer of truth is thoroughly obscured. It's no wonder how quickly they lose all grip on reality!"

"And that's what you told them?"

He stood in his dressing gown staring down at a Square and gardens even BBIC had failed to conquer. The trees were full of the nests crows had built since the first farmers hedged the meadow. His study, with its books and big old-fashioned stereo, had hardly changed but had a deserted air now.

I had brought the ingredients of our lunch and stood in my street clothes with my bag expecting him to lead me to the kitchen, but he remained in his window and wanted me to stay. He pointed mysteriously towards the Duke's Elm and Gilbert's War Memorial, a fanciful drinking fountain that had never worked.

"That's what I told them, my dear. In the pulpit first. Then in the travelling shows. Then on the street. I was arrested for obstruction in 1937, refused to recognise the court and refused to pay the fine. This was my first brief prison sentence. Eventually I got myself in solitary.

"When I left prison I saw a London even more wretched than before. Beggars were everywhere. Vagrants were not in those days tolerated in the West End, but were still permitted in the doorways of Soho and Somers Town. The squalor was as bad as anything Mayhew reported. I thought my anger had been brought under control in prison but I was wrong. The obscene exploitation of the weak by the strong was everywhere displayed. I did whatever I could. I stood on a box at Speaker's Corner. I wrote and printed pamphlets. I sent letters and circulars to everyone, to the newspapers, to the BBC. Nobody took me very seriously. In the main I was ignored. When I was not ignored I was insulted. Eventually, holding a sign in Oxford Street, I was again arrested but this time there was a scuffle with the arresting policeman. I went into Wormwood Scrubs until the outbreak of the Blitz when I was released to volunteer for the ambulance service. Well, I wasn't prepared to return to prison after the War and in fact my ideas had gained a certain currency. Do you remember what Londoners were like then, my dear? After we learned how to look after ourselves rather better than our leaders could? Our morale was never higher. London's last war was a war the people won in spite of the authorities. But somewhere along the line we gave our achievements over to the politicians, the power addicts. The result is that we now live in rookeries and slum courts almost as miserable as our 19th century ancestors', or exist in blanketed luxury as divorced from common experience as a Russian Tsar. I'm not entirely sure about the quality of that progress, are you? These days the lowest common denominators are sought for as if they were principles."

"You're still an example to us," I said, thinking to console him.

He was grateful but shook his head, still looking down at the old elm as if he hoped to see someone there. "I'll never be sure if I did any good. For a while, you know, I was quite a celebrity until they realised I wasn't offering an anti-Christian message and then they mostly lost interest. I couldn't get on with those Jesuits they all cultivated. But I spoke to the Fabians twice and met Wells, Shaw, Priestley and the rest. I was very cheerful. It appeared that I was spreading my message. I didn't understand that I was merely a vogue. I was quite a favourite with Bloomsbury and there was talk of putting me on Radio Luxembourg. But gradually doors were closed to me and I was rather humiliated on a couple of occasions. I hadn't started all this for fame or approval, so as soon as I realised what was happening I retired to the travelling shows and seaside fairgrounds which proliferated in England in the days before television.

"Eventually I began to doubt the value of my own pronouncements, since my audiences were dwindling and an evil force was progressing unchecked across Europe. We faced a future dominated by a few cruel dictatorships. Some kind of awful war was inevitable. During my final spell in clink I made up my mind to keep my thoughts to myself and consider better ways of getting them across. I saw nothing wrong with the message, but assumed myself to be a bad medium. In my free time I went out into the Square as much as I could. It was still easy to think there, even during the War."

He took a step towards the window, almost as if he had seen someone he recognized and then he shrugged, turning his head away sharply and pretending to take an interest in one of his Sickerts. "I found her there first, as you know, in 1933. And that one sight of her inspired a whole series of sermons. I came back week after week, but it always seemed as if I had just missed her. You could say I was in love with her. I wanted desperately for her to be real. Well, I had seen her again the evening I was 'unfrocked'. Of course I was in a pretty terrible state. I was praying. Since a boy I've always found it easy to pray in the Square. I identified God with the Duke's Elm—or at least I visualised God as a powerful old tree. I never understood why we placed such peculiar prohibitions on how we represented God. That's what they mean by 'pagan'. It has nothing to do with one's intellectual sophistication. I was praying when she appeared for the second time. First there was that strong scent of roses. When I looked up I saw her framed against the great trunk and it seemed a rose drew all her branches, leaves and blooms together and took human form!"

His face had a slight flush as he spoke. "It seemed to me I'd been given a companion to help me make the best use of my life. She had that vibrancy, that uncommon beauty; she was a sentient flower.

"Various church examiners to whom I explained the vision understood my Rose either as an expression of my own unstable mind or as a manifestation of the devil. It was impossible for me to see her as either.

"She stepped forward and held out her hand to me. I had difficulty distinguishing her exact colours. They were many and subtle—an unbroken haze of pink and green and pale gold—all the shades of the rose. Her figure was slim but it wasn't easy to tell where her clothes met her body or even which was which. Her eyes changed in the light from deep emerald to violet. In spite of her extraordinary aura of power, her manner was almost hesitant. I think I was weeping as I went to her. I probably asked her what I should do. I know I decided to continue with my work. It was years before I saw her again, after I'd come out of prison for the last time."

"But you did see her again?"

"Many times. Especially during the Blitz. But I'd learned my lesson. I kept all that to myself."

"You were afraid of prison?"

"If you like. But I think it was probably more positive. God granted me a dream of the universe and her ever-expanding realities and I helped in the procreation of the new messiah!"

I waited for him to continue but he turned from the window with a broad smile. He was exhausted, tottering a little as he came with me to the kitchen and sat down in my place while I began to cook. He chatted amiably about the price of garlic and I prepared the dishes as he had taught me years before. This time, however, I was determined to encourage him to talk about himself.

He took a second glass of wine, his cheeks a little pinker than usual, his hair already beginning to rise about his head in a pure white fog.

"I suppose I needed her most during the War. There wasn't much time for talk, but I still came out to the Duke's Elm to pray. We began to meet frequently, always in the evenings before dark, and would walk together, comparing experience. She was from a quite different world—although her world sort of included ours. Eventually we became lovers."

"Did she have a name?"

"I think so. I called her the Rose. I travelled with her. She took me to paradise, my dear, nowhere less! She showed me the whole of Creation! And so after a while my enthusiasm returned. Again, I wanted to share my vision but I had become far more cautious. I had a suspicion that I made a mistake the first time and almost lost my Rose as a result. When my nephew, who was in BBC Talks, offered me a new pulpit I was pretty much ready for it. This time I was determined to keep the reality to myself and just apply what I had experienced to ordinary, daily life. The public could not accept the intensity and implications of my pure vision. I cultivated an avuncularity which probably shocked those who knew me well. I became quite the jolly Englishman! I was offered speaking engagements in America. I was such a show-off. I spent less and less time in the Square and eventually months passed before I realised that I had lost contact with my Rose and our child! I felt such an utter fool, my dear. As soon as I understood what was happening I gave everything up. But it was too late."

"You haven't seen her since?"

"Only in dreams."

"What do you believe she was? The spirit of the tree?" I did my best to seem matter-of-fact, but he knew what I was up to and laughed, pouring himself more wine.

"She is her own spirit, my dear, make no mistake."

And then the first course was ready, a *paté de foie gras* made by my friend Loris Murrail in Paris. Begg agreed that it was as good as his own. For our main course we had Quantock veal in saffron. He ate it with appreciative relish. He had not been able to cook much lately, he said, and his appetite was reduced, but he enjoyed every bite. I was touched by his enthusiasm and made a private decision to come regularly again. Cooking him lunch would be my way of giving him something back. My spirits rose at the prospect and it was only then that I realised how much I had missed his company.

"Perhaps," he said, "she was sent to me to sustain me only when I most needed her. I had thought it a mistake to try to share her with the world. I never spoke of her again after I had told the bishop about her and was accused of militant paganism, primitive nature-worship. I saw his point of view but I always worshipped God in all his manifestations. The bishop seemed to argue that paganism was indistinguishable from common experience and therefore could not be considered a religion at all!"

"You worshipped her?"

"In a sense, my dear. As a man worships his wife."

I had made him a *tiesen sinamon* and he took his time with the meringue, lifting it up to his lips on the delicate silver fork which Begg's Cotswold benches had produced for Liberty in 1903. "I don't know if it's better or worse, dear, but the world is changing profoundly you know. Our methods of making it safe just aren't really working any more. The danger of the simple answer is always with us and is inclined to lead to some sort of Final Solution. We are affected by turbulence as a leaf in the wind, but still we insist that the best way of dealing with the fact is to deny it or ignore it. And so we go on, hopelessly attempting to contain the thunder and the lightning and creating only further confusion! We're always caught by surprise! Yet it would require so little, surely, in the way of courage and imagination to find a way out, especially with today's wonderful computers?"

I had been depressed by the level and the outcome of the recent British election and was not optimistic. He agreed. "How we love to cling to the wrecks which took us onto the rocks in the first place. In our panic we don't even see the empty lifeboats within easy swimming distance."

He did not have the demeanour of a disappointed prophet. He remained lively and humorous. There was no sense of defeat about him, rather of quiet victory, of conquered pain. He did not at first seem disposed to tell me any more but when were having coffee a casual remark set him off on a train of thought which led naturally back to that most significant event of his life. "We aren't flawed," he said, "just as God isn't flawed. What we perceive as flaws are a reflection of our own failure to see the whole." He spoke of a richly populated multiverse which was both within us and outside us. "We're all reflections and echoes, one of another, and our originals, dear, are lost, probably forever. That was what I understood from my vision. I wrote it in my journal. Perhaps, very rarely, we're granted a glimpse of God's entire plan? Perhaps only when our need is desperate. I have no doubt that God sent me my Rose."

I am still of a secular disposition. "Or perhaps," I suggested, "as God you sent yourself a vision?"

He did not find this blasphemous but neither did he think it worth pursuing. "It's much of muchness, that," he said.

He was content in his beliefs. He had questioned them once but now he was convinced. "God sent me a vision and I followed her. She was made flesh. A miracle. I went with her to where she lived, in the fields of colour, in the far ether. We were married. We gave birth to a new human creature, neither male nor female but self-reproducing, a new messiah, and it set us free at last to dwell on that vast multiplicity of the heavens, to contemplate a quasi-infinity of versions of ourselves, our histories, our experience. That was what God granted me, my dear, when he sent me my Rose. Perhaps I was the antichrist, after all, or at least its parent."

"In your vision did you see what became of the child?"

He spoke with lighthearted familiarity, not recalling some distant dream but describing an immediate reality. "Oh, yes. It grew to lead the world upon a new stage in our evolution. I'm not sure you'd believe the details, my dear, or find them very palatable."

I smiled at this, but for the first time in my life felt a hint of profound terror and I suppressed a sudden urge to shout at him, to tell him how ridiculous I considered his visions, a bizarre blend of popular prophecy and alchemical mumbo-jumbo which even a New Age traveller would take with a pinch of E. My anger overwhelmed me. Though I regained control of it he recognised it. He continued to speak but with growing reluctance and perhaps melancholy. "I saw a peculiar inevitability to the process. What, after all, do most of us live for? Ourselves? And what use is that? What value? What profit?"

With a great sigh he put down his fork. "That was delicious." His satisfaction felt to me like an accolade.

"You're only describing human nature." I took his plate.

"Is that what keeps us on a level with the amoeba, my dear, and makes us worth about as much individual affection? Come now! We allow ourselves to be ruled by every brutish, greedy instinct, not by what is significantly human in our nature! Our imagination is our greatest gift. It gives us our moral sensibility." He looked away through the dining room window at the glittering domes of Gautier House and in the light the lines of his face were suddenly emphasised.

I had no wish ever to quarrel with him again. The previous argument, we were agreed, had cost us both too much. But I had to say what I thought. "I was once told the moment I mentioned morality was the moment I'd crossed the line into lunacy," I said. "I suppose we must agree to understand things differently."

For once he had forgotten his usual courtesy. I don't think he heard me. "Wasn't all this damage avoidable?" he murmured. "Weren't there ways in which cities could have grown up as we grew up, century adding to century, style to style, wisdom to wisdom? Isn't there something seriously wrong with the cycle we're in? Isn't there some way out?"

I made to reply but he shook his head, his hands on the table. "I saw her again, you know, several times after the birth. How beautiful she was! How much beauty she showed me! It's like an amplification, my dear, of every sense! A discovery of new senses. An understanding that we don't need to discard anything as long as we continue to learn from it. It isn't frightening what she showed me. It's perfectly familiar once you begin to see. It's like looking at the quintessential versions of our ordinary realities. Trees, animals—they're there, in essence. You begin to discover all that. The fundamental geometry's identified. Well, you've seen this new math, haven't you?"

He seemed so vulnerable at that moment that for once I wasn't frank. I was unconvinced by what I judged as hippy physics made possible only by the new creative powers of computers. I didn't offer him an argument.

"You can't help but hope that it's what death is like," he said. "You become an angel."

He got up and returned slowly to his dusty study, beckoning me to look out with him into the twilight gathering around the trees where crows croaked their mutual reassurances through the darkening air. He glanced only once towards the old elm then turned his head away sharply. "You'll think this unlikely, I know, but we first came together physically at midnight under a full moon as bright and thin and yellow as honesty in a dark blue sky. I looked at the moon through those strong black branches the moment before we touched. The joy of our union was indescribable. It was a confirmation of my faith. I made a mistake going back into public life. What good did it do for anyone, my dear?"

"We all made too many easy assumptions," I said. "It wasn't your fault."

"I discovered sentimental solutions and comforted myself with them. Those comforts I turned to material profit. They became lies. And I lost her, my dear." He made a small, anguished gesture. "I'm still waiting for her to come back."

He was scarcely aware of me. I felt I had intruded upon a private moment and suggested that I had tired him and should leave. Looking at me in surprise but without dispute he came towards me, remarking in particular on the saffron sauce. "I can't tell you how much it meant to me, my dear, in every way."

I promised to return the following Wednesday and cook. He licked his pink lips in comic anticipation and seemed genuinely delighted by the prospect. "Yum, yum." He embraced me suddenly with his frail body, his sweet face staring blindly into mine.

I had found his last revelations disturbing and my tendency was to dismiss them perhaps as an early sign of his senility. I even considered putting off my promised visit, but was already planning the next lunch when three days later I took a call from Mrs. Arthur Begg who kept an eye on him and had my number. The Clapham Antichrist had died in his sleep. She had found him at noon with his head raised upon his massive pillows, the light from the open window falling on his face. She enthused over his wonderful expression in death.

In memorium, Horst Grimm

THE OPIUM GENERAL

The Opium General

They had lived in a kind of besieged darkness for several weeks. At first she had welcomed the sense of solitude after the phone was cut off. They ignored the front door unless friends knew the secret knock. It was almost security, behind the blinds. From his ugly anxiety Charlie had calmed for a while but had soon grown morose and accusatory. There were too many creditors. The basement flat turned into a prison he was afraid to leave. When she had arrived three years ago it had seemed a treasure house; now she saw it merely as a record of his unrealized dreams: his half-read books, his comics, his toys, his synthesizers no longer stimulated him yet he refused to get rid of a single broken model Spitfire. They were tokens of his former substance, of a glorious past. When she suggested they go for a walk he said: "Too many people know me in Notting Hill." He meant the customers he had burned, taking money for drugs he never delivered, and the important dealers he had never paid. He tried to form a unity of his many frustrations: a general pattern, a calculated plot against him. A friend was murdered in a quarrel over sulphate at a house in Talbot Road. He decided the knife had been meant for him. "I've made too many enemies." This was his self-pitying phase.

She steered him as best as she could away from paranoia. She was frightened by overt instability, but had learned to feel relaxed so long as the signs were unadmitted, buried. In response to her nervousness he pulled himself together in the only way he knew: the appropriate image. He said it was time for a stiff upper lip, for holding the thin red line. She was perfectly satisfied, her sympathy for him was restored and she had been able to keep going. He became like Leslie Howard in an old war film. She tried to find somebody who could help him. This awful uncertainty stopped him doing his best. If he got clear, got a bit of money, they could start afresh. He wanted to write a novel: in Inverness, he thought, where he had worked in a hotel. Once away she could calm him down, get him to be his old self. But there remained the suspicion he might still choose madness as his escape. His friends said he habitually put himself into mental hospitals where he need feel no personal responsibility. He said, though, that it was chemical.

"Nobody's after you, Charlie, really." She had spent hours trying to win round all the big dealers. She went to see some of them on her own. They assured her with dismissive disgust that they had written off his debts and forgotten about him but would never do business with him again. The landlord was trying to serve them with a summons for almost a year's unpaid rent and had been unnecessarily rude the last time she had appealed to him. She blamed herself. She had longed for a return of the euphoria of their first weeks together. There had been plenty of money then, or at least credit. She had deliberately shut out the voice of her own common sense. In her drugged passivity she let him convince her something concrete would come of his elaborate fantasies; she lent her own considerable manipulative powers to his, telling his bank-manager of all the record-companies who were after his work, of the planned tour, of the ex-agent who owed him a fortune. This lifted him briefly and he became the tall handsome red-headed insouciant she had first met. "Partners in bullshit," he said cheerfully. "You should be on the stage, Ellie. You can be a star in my next road-show." It had been his apparent good humoured carelessness in the face of trouble which made him seem so attractive to her three years ago when she left home to live here. She had not realized nobody in the music business would work with him any more, not even on sessions, because he got so loony. It was nerves, she knew, but he could be so rude to her, to everybody, and make a terrible impression. At the very last guest spot he had done, in Dingwalls, the roadies deliberately sabotaged his sound because he had been so overbearing. As Jimmy had told her gravely later: "Ye canna afford to get up the roadies' noses, Ellie. They can make or break a set." Jimmy Begg had been Charlie's partner in their first psychedelic group, but had split the third time Charlie got himself in the bin. It was a bad sign, Jimmy told her, when Charlie started wearing his "army suit", as he had done to the Dingwalls gig.

Over the past two weeks Charlie had worn his uniform all the time. It seemed to make him feel better. "Look out for snipers, Algy," he warned her when she went shopping. He kept the shutters of the front room windows closed, lay in the bed all day and stayed up at night rolling himself cigarettes and fiddling with his little Casio synthesizer. He needed R&R, he said. When, through tiredness, she had snapped at him not to be so silly, playing at soldiers, he turned away from her sorrowfully: a military martyr, a decent Englishman forced into the dirty business of war. "This isn't any fun for any of us." His father had been a regular sergeant in the Royal Artillery and had always wanted Charlie to go to Sandhurst. His parents were in Africa now, running a Bulawayo grocery shop. He frequently addressed her as sergeant-major. Creditors became "the enemy"; he needed more troops, reinforcements, fresh supplies. "What about a cup of coffee, s'a'rnt-major?" and she would have to get up to make him one. His old friends found the role familiar. They didn't help by playing up to it. "How's the general?" they would ask. He got out his military prints, his badges, his model soldiers, his aircraft charts. They were on every wall and surface now. He read Biggles books and old copies of *The Eagle.*

His last phone call had been to Gordon in Camden. "Morning to you, field marshal. Spot of bother at this end. Pinned down under fire. Troops needing supplies. What can you get to us?" Gordon, his main coke-supplier, told him to fuck himself. "The chap's gone over to the enemy," Charlie was almost crying. "Turned yellow. Made of the wrong bally stuff." She pushed her long pale hair away from her little oval face and begged him to talk normally. "Nobody's going to take you seriously if you put on a funny voice."

"Can't think what you mean, old thing." He straightened his black beret on his cropped head. He had always been vain but now he spent fifty percent of his waking time in front of the mirror. "Don't tell me you're crackin', too." He rode his motorbike to Brixton and came back with cash, claiming he had been cheated on the price. "We're going to have transport and logistics problems for a bit, s'a'rnt-major. But we'll get by somehow, eh? Darkest before the dawn and so on." She had just begun to warm to his courage when he gloomily added: "But I suppose you'll go AWOL next. One simply can't get the quality of front-line chap." All his other girl-friends had finally been unable to take him. She swore she was not the same. She made him a cup of tea and told him to go to bed and rest: her own universal remedy. It always seemed to work for her. Dimly she recognized his desperate reaching for certainties and order, yet his "general" was slowly wearing her down. She asked her mother to come to stay with her for a couple of days. "You should be on your own, love," said her mother. She was discomfited by Charlie's role. "Get yourself a little place. A job."

Ellie spread her short fingers on the table and stared at them. She was numb all over. He had made her senses flare like a firework; now she felt spent. She looked dreadful, said her mother. She was too thin, she was wearing too much make-up and perfume. Charlie liked it she said. "He's not doing you any good love. The state of you!" All this in a murmur, while Charlie napped in the next room.

"I can't let him down now." Ellie polished her nails. "Everybody owes him money." But she knew she was both too frightened to leave and felt obscurely that she had given him more than his due, that he owed her for something. There was nobody else to support her; she was worn out. It was up to him. She would get him on his feet again, then he would in turn help her.

"You'd be better off at home," said her mother doubtfully. "Dad's a lot calmer than he used to be." Her father hated Charlie. The peculiar thing was they were very much alike in a lot of ways. Her father looked back with nostalgia to wartime and his Tank Regiment.

She and her mother went up to Tesco's together. The Portobello Road was crowded as usual, full of black women with prams and shopping bags, Pakistani women in saris, clutching at the hands of two or three kids, old hippies in big miserable coats, Irish drunks, gypsies, a smattering of middle-class women from the other side of Ladbroke Grove. Her mother hated the street; she wanted them to move somewhere more respectable. They pushed the cart round the supermarket. "At least you've got your basics for a bit," she said. She was a tiny, harassed woman with a face permanently masked, an ear permanently deaf to anything but the most conventional statements. "Bring Charlie to Worthing for a couple of weeks. It'll do you both good." But Charlie knew, as well as anyone, that he and Ellie's dad would be at loggerheads within a day. "Got to stay at H.Q." he said. "Position could improve any moment." He was trying to write new lyrics for Jimmy's band, but they kept coming out the same as those they'd done together ten years before, about war and nuclear bombs and cosmic soldiers. Her mother returned to Worthing with a set, melancholy face, her shoulders rounded by thirty years of dogged timidity. Ellie noticed her own shoulders were becoming hunched, too. She made an effort to straighten them and then heard in her mind Charlie (or was it her dad?) saying "back straight, stomach in" and she let herself slump again. This self-defeating defiance was the only kind she dared allow herself. Her long hair (which Charlie insisted she keep) dragged her head to the ground.

That night he burned all his lyrics. "Top Secret documents," he called them. When she begged him to stop, saying somebody would buy them surely, he rounded on her. "If you're so into money, why don't you go out and earn some?" She was afraid to leave him to his own devices. He might do anything while she was away. He'd have a new girl-friend in five minutes. He couldn't stand being alone. She had thought him sensitive and vulnerable when he courted her. They met in a pub near The Music Machine. He seemed so interested in her, at once charmingly bold, shy and attentive. He made her laugh. She had mothered him a bit, she supposed. She would have done anything for him. Could that have been a mistake?

"You've got to find out what you want," said her sluttish friend Joan, who lived with an ex-biker. "Be independent." Joan worked at the health-food shop and was into feminism. "Don't let any fucking feller mess you around. Be your own woman." But Joan was bisexual and had her eye on Ellie. Her objectivity couldn't be trusted. Joan was having trouble with her old man yet she didn't seem about to split.

"I don't know who I am." Ellie stared at the Victorian screen Charlie had bought her. It had pictures of Lancers and Guardsman varnished brownish yellow. "I was reading. We all define ourselves through other people, don't we?"

"Not as much as you do, dearie," said Joan. "What about a holiday? I'm thinking of staying at this cottage in Wales next month. We could both do with a break away from blokes."

Ellie said she'd think about it. She now spent most of her time in the kitchen looking out at the tiny overgrown yard. She made up lists in her mind: lists of things they could sell, lists of outfits she could buy, lists of places she would like to visit, lists of people who might be able to help Charlie. She had a list of their debts in a drawer somewhere. She considered a list of musicians and A&R men they knew. But these days all Charlie had that people wanted was dope contacts. And nobody would let him have as much as a joint on credit any more. It was disgusting. People kept in touch because you could help them score. The minute you weren't useful, they dropped you. Charlie wouldn't let her say this, though. He said it was her fault. She turned friends against him. "Why don't you fuck off, too? You've had everything I've got." But when she began to pack (knowing she could not leave) he told her he needed her. She was all he had left. He was sorry for being a bastard.

"I think I'm bad luck for you." Really she meant something else which she was too afraid to let into her consciousness. He was weak and selfish. She had stood by him through everything. But possibly he was right to blame her. She had let herself be entranced by his wit, his smiling mouth, his lean, nervous body so graceful in repose, so awkward when he tried to impress. She should have brought him down to earth sooner. She had known it was going wrong, but had believed something must turn up to save them. "Can't we go away?" she asked him early one afternoon. The room was in semi-darkness. Sun fell on the polished pine of the table between them; a single beam from the crack in the shutters. "What about that mate of yours in Tangier?" She picked unconsciously at the brocade chair left by his ex-wife. She felt she had retreated behind a wall which was her body, painted, shaved, perfumed: a lie of sexuality and compliance. She had lost all desire.

"And have the enemy seize the flat while we're there? You've got to remember, sergeant-major, that possession is nine-tenths of the law." He lay in his red Windsor rocker. He wore nothing but army gear, with a big belt around his waist, a sure sign of his insecurity. He drew his reproduction Luger from its holster and checked its action with profound authority. She stared at the reddish hair on his thick wrists, at the flaking spots on his fingers which resembled the early stages of a disease. His large, flat cheekbones seemed inflamed; there were huge bags under his eyes. He was almost forty. He was fighting off mortality as ferociously as he fought off what he called "the mundane world". She continued in an abstracted way to feel sorry for him. She still thought, occasionally, of Leslie Howard in the trenches. "Then couldn't we spend a few days on Vince's houseboat?"

"Vince has retreated to Shropshire. A non-pukkah wallah," he said sardonically. He and Vince had often played Indian army officers. "His old lady's given him murder. Shouldn't have taken her aboard. Women always let you down in a crunch." He glanced away.

She was grateful for the flush of anger which pushed her to her feet and carried her into the kitchen. "You ungrateful bastard. You should have kept your bloody dick in your trousers then, shouldn't you!" She became afraid, but it was not the old immediate terror of a blow, it was a sort of dull expectation of pain. She was seized with contempt for her own dreadful judgement. She sighed, waiting for him to respond in anger. She turned. He looked miserably at his Luger and reholstered it. He stood up, plucking at his khaki creases, patting at his webbing. He straightened his beret in front of the mirror, clearing his throat. He was pale. "What about organizing some tiffin, sergeant-major?"

"I'll go out and get the bread." She took the Scottish pound note from the tin on the mantelpiece.

"Don't be long. The enemy could attack at any time." For a second he looked genuinely frightened. He was spitting a little when he spoke. His hair needed washing. He was normally so fussy about his appearance but he hadn't bathed properly in days. She had not dared say anything.

She went up the basement steps. Powys Square was noisy with children playing Cowboys and Indians. They exasperated her. She was twenty-five and felt hundreds of years older than them, than Charlie, than her mum and dad. Perhaps I'm growing up, she thought as she turned into Portobello Road and stopped outside the baker's. She stared at the loaves, pretending to choose. She looked at the golden bread and inhaled the sweet warmth; she looked at her reflection in the glass. She wore her tailored skirt, silk blouse, stockings, lacey bra and panties. He usually liked her to be feminine, but sometimes preferred her as a tomboy. "It's the poofter in me." She wasn't sure what she should be wearing now. A uniform like his? But it would be a lie. She looked at herself again. It was all a lie. Then she turned away from the baker's and walked on, past stalls of avocados and Savoys, tomatoes and oranges, to the pawn shop where two weeks ago she had given up her last treasures. She paid individual attention to each electronic watch and every antique ring in the window and saw nothing she wanted. She crossed the road. Finch's pub was still open. Black men lounged in the street drinking from bottles, engaged in conventional badinage; she hoped nobody would recognize her. She went down Elgin Crescent, past the newsagent where she owed money, into the cherry-and-apple-blossom of the residential streets. The blossom rose around her high heels like a sudden tide. Its colour, pink and white, almost blinded her. She breathed heavily. The scent came as if through a filter, no longer consoling. Feeling faint she sat on a low wall outside somebody's big house, her shopping bag and purse in her left hand, her right hand stroking mechanically at the rough concrete, desperate for sensation. Ordinary feeling was all she wanted. She could not imagine where it had gone. An ordinary life. She saw her own romanticism as a rotting tooth capped with gold. Her jaw ached. She looked upwards through the blossom at the blue sky in which sharply-defined white clouds moved very slowly towards the sun, like cut-outs on a stage. She became afraid, wanting to turn back: she must get the bread before the scene ended and the day became grey again. But she needed this peace so badly. She grew self-conscious as a swarthy youth in a cheap black velvet suit went by whistling to himself. With only a little effort she could have made him attractive, but she no longer had the energy. Panic made her heart beat. Charlie could go over the top any minute. He might stack all the furniture near the doors and windows, as he had done once, or decide to rewire his equipment (he was useless at practical jobs) and be throwing a fit, breaking things, blaming her because a fuse had blown. Or he might be out in the street trying to get a reaction from a neighbour, baiting them, insulting them, trying to charm them. Or he might be at the Princess Alexandra, looking for somebody who would trust him with the money for a gram of coke or half-a-g of smack and stay put until closing time when he promised to return: restoring his ego, as he sometimes did, with a con-trick. If so he could be in real trouble. Everyone said he'd been lucky so far. She forgot the bread and hurried back.

The children were still yelling and squealing as she turned into the square in time to see him walking away round the opposite corner of the building. He was dressed in his combat beret, his flying jacket, his army-boots, his sun-glasses. He had his toy Luger and his sheath-knife on his belt. Trembling, she went down the steps of the basement, put her key in his front door, turned it, stepped inside. The whole of the front room was in confusion, as if he had been searching for something. The wicker chair had been turned over. The bamboo table was askew. As she straightened it (for she was automatically neat) she saw a note. He had used a model jeep as a weight. She screwed the note up. She went into the kitchen and put the kettle on. Waiting for the kettle to boil she flattened the paper on the draining board:

1400 hrs. Duty calls. Instructions from HQ to proceed at once to battle-zone. Will contact at duration of hostilities. Trust nobody. Hold the fort.

—BOLTON, C-in-C, Sector Six.

Her legs shook as she crossed back to the tea-pot. Within three or four days he would probably be in a police-station or a mental hospital. He would opt to become a voluntary patient. He had surrendered.

Her whole body shook now, with relief, with a sense of her own failure. He had won, after all. He could always win. She returned to the front door and slowly secured the bolts at top and bottom. She pushed back the shutters. Carefully she made herself a cup of tea and sat at the table with her chin in her hand staring through the bars of the basement window. The tea grew cold, but she continued to sip at it. She was out of the contest. She awaited her fate.

THE CAIRENE PURSE

The Cairene Purse

1 : Her First Fond Hope Of Eden Blighted

On the edge of the Nile's fertile shadow, pyramids merged with the desert and from the air seemed almost two-dimensional in the steady light of late morning. Spreading now beyond the town of Giza, Cairo's forty million people threatened to engulf, with their old automobiles, discarded electronics and every dusty non-degradable of the modern world, the grandiose tombs of their ancestors.

Though Cairo, like Calcutta, was a monument to the enduring survival of our race, I was glad to leave. I had spent only as much time as I needed, seeking information about my archaeologist sister and discovering that everyone in the academic community thought she had returned to England at least a year ago. The noise had begun to seem as tangible as the haze of sand which hung over the crowded motorways, now a mass of moving flesh, of camels, donkeys, horses, mules and humans hauling every variety of vehicle and cargo, with the occasional official electric car or, even rarer, petrol-driven truck.

I suppose it had been a tribute to my imagined status that I had been given a place on a plane, rather than having to take the river or the weekly train to Aswan. Through the porthole of the little VW8 everything but the Nile and its verdant borders were the colours of sand, each shade and texture of which still held meaning for the nomad Arab, the Bedouin who had conquered the First Kingdom and would conquer several others down the millennia. In the past only the Ptolomies, turning their backs on the Nile and the Sahara, ever truly lost the sources of Egypt's power.

My main reason for accepting the assignment was personal rather than professional. My sister had not written for some months and her letters before that had been disconnected, hinting at some sort of emotional disturbance, perhaps in connection with the dig on which I knew she had been working. An employee of UNEC, I had limited authority in Egypt and did not expect to discover any great mysteries at Lake Nasser, which continued to be the cause of unusual weather. The dam's builders somewhat typically had refused to anticipate this. They had also been warned by our people in the 1950s that the New High Dam would eventually so poison the river with bilharzia that anyone using its water would die. The rain, some of it acid, had had predictable effects, flooding quarries and washing away towns. The local Nubians had long since been evicted from their valleys to make way for the lake. Their new settlements, traditionally built, had not withstood the altered environment, so the government had thrown up concrete shells for them. The road to Aswan from the airport was lined with bleak, half-built structures of rusted metal girders and cinder blocks. Today's Egyptians paid a high price for regulated water.

From the airport my horse-drawn taxi crossed the old English dam with its sluices and gigantic gauges, a Victorian engineer's dream of mechanical efficiency, and began the last lap of the journey into town. Aswan, wretched as much of it is, has a magic few Nile settlements now possess, rising from the East Bank to dominate the coppery blue waters and glinting granite islands of the wide river where white-sailed feluccas cruise gracefully back and forth, ferrying tourists and townspeople between the two sides. The heights, massive grey boulders, are commanded by a beautiful park full of old eucalyptus, poplars and monkey-puzzle trees. Above this, the stately Edwardian glory of Cook's Cataract Hotel is a marvellous example of balconied and shuttered rococco British orientalism at its finest.

The further up river one goes the poorer Aswan becomes, though even here the clapboard and corrugated iron, the asbestos sheeting and crumbling mud walls are dominated by a splendid hill-top mosque in the grand Turkish style. I had asked to be billeted at a modest hotel in the middle of town, near the Souk. From the outside, the Hotel Osiris, with its pale pink and green pseudo-neon, reminded me of those backstreet Marseilles hotels where once you could take your partner for a few francs an hour. It had the same romantic attraction, the same impossible promises. I found that, once within its tiny fly-thick lobby—actually the communal hallway leading directly to the courtyard—I was as lost to its appeal as any pop to his lid. I had discovered a temporary spiritual home.

The Osiris, though scarcely more than a bed and breakfast place by London standards, boasted four or five porters, all of them eager to take my bag to the rooms assigned me by a Hindu lady at the desk. I let one carry my canvas grip up two flights of dirty stairs to a little tiled, run-down apartment looking into the building's central well where two exhausted dogs, still coupled, panted on their sides in the heat. Giving him a five-pound note, I asked my porter on the off-chance if he had heard of an Englishwoman called Noone or von Bek living in Aswan. My sister had used the *poste restante* and, when I had last been here, there were few Europeans permanently living in town. He regretted that he could not help. He would ask his brother, who had been in Aswan several months. Evidently, now that I had as it were paid for the information in advance he felt obliged to me. The *bakshish* custom is usually neither one of bribery nor begging in any

European sense, but has a fair amount to do with smooth social intercourse. There is always, with legitimate *bakshish*, an exchange. Some measure of mutual respect is also usual. Most Arabs place considerable emphasis on good manners and are not always tolerant of European coarseness.

I had last been in Egypt long before the great economic convulsion following that chain-reaction of destruction or near-exhaustion of so many resources. Then Aswan had been the final port of call for the millions of tourists who cruised the Nile from dawn to dusk, the sound of their dance music, the smell of their barbecues, drifting over fields and mud villages which had remained unchanged for five thousand years.

In the 80s and 90s of the last century Aswan had possessed, among others, a Hilton, a Sheraton, a Ritz-Carlton and a Holiday Inn, but now the luckiest local families had requisitioned the hotels and only the State-owned Cataract remained, a place of pilgrimage for every wealthy enthusiast of 1930s detective stories or autobiographies of the 20th century famous. Here, during wartime, secret meetings had been held and mysterious bargains struck between unlikely participants. Today on the water below the terrace some tourists still sailed, the Israelis and the Saudis on their own elegant schoomers, while other boats carried mixtures of Americans, Italians and Germans, French, English, Swedes, Spaniards, Japanese and Hungarians, their women dressed and painted like pagan temptresses of the local soap-operas, displaying their bodies naked on the sundecks of vast slow-moving windliners the size of an earlier era's ocean-going ships, serving to remind every decent Moslem exactly what the road to Hell looked like. No 18th century English satirist could have provided a better image.

As an officer of the UN's Conservation and Preservation Department I knew all too well how little of Egypt's monuments were still visible, how few existed in any recognisable state. Human erosion, the dam raising the water-table, the volume of garbage casually dumped in the river, the activities of archaeologists and others, of tourists encouraged in their millions to visit the great sites and bring their hard currency, the two-year Arabian war, all had created a situation where those monuments still existing were banned to everyone but the desperate restorers. Meanwhile replicas had been made by the Disney Corporation and located in distant desert settlements surrounded by vacation towns, artificial trees and vast swimming pools, built by French and German experts and named "Rameses City", "Land of the Gods" or "Tutankhamen World". I was sure that this was why my sister had been secretive about her team's discoveries, why it was important to try to avoid the circumstances which now made Abu Simbel little more than a memory of two great engineering miracles.

When I had washed and changed I left the Osiris and strolled through busy evening alleys in the direction of the corniche, the restored Victorian riverfront promenade which reminded me more than anywhere of the old ocean boulevard at Yalta. Without her earlier weight of tourists, Aswan had developed a lazy, decayed glamour. The foodstalls, the fake antiquities, the flimsy headdresses and *gelabeas* sold as traditional costume, the souvenir shops and postcard stands, the "cafetrias" offering "Creme Teas" and "Mix Grile", were still patronised by a few plump Poles and tomato-coloured English who had been replaced in the main by smaller numbers of blond East Africans, Swedes and Nigerians affecting the styles and mannerisms of thirty or forty years earlier and drawn here, I had heard, by a Holy Man on the outskirts of Aswan who taught a peculiar mixture of orthodox Sunni Islam and his own brand of mysticism which accepted the creeds of Jews and Christians as well as the existence of other planetary populations, and spoke of a "pure" form of Islam practised in other parts of the galaxy.

Aswan's latter-day hippies, wearing the fashions of my own youthful parents, gave me a queer feeling at first, for although Egypt offers several experiences akin to time-travel, these images of recent history, perhaps of a happier period altogether, were somehow more incongruous than a broken down VW, for instance, being dragged behind a disgusted camel. There was a greater preponderance of charm-sellers and fortune-tellers than I remembered, together with blank-eyed European men and women, some of them with babies or young children, who begged me for drug-money on the street. With the rise of Islamic-Humanism, the so-called Arab Enlightenment, coupled to the increasing power of North Africa and the Middle East in world politics, the drug laws, introduced originally to placate foreign tour operators and their governments, had been relaxed or formally abolished. Aswan, I had heard, was now some kind of Mecca for privileged youngsters and visionary artists, much as Haight Ashbury or Ladbroke Grove had been in the 1960s. Romanticism of that heady, exaggerated, rather mystical variety was once again loose in the world and the comforts it offered seemed to me almost like devilish temptations. But I was of that puritanical, judgemental generation which had rejected the abstractions of its parents in favour of more realistic, as we saw it, attitudes. A good many of us had virtually rejected the entire Western Enlightenment itself and retreated into a kind of liberal mediaevalism not incompatible with large parts of the Arab world. In my own circles I was considered something of a radical.

I had to admit however that I found these new Aswanians attractive. In many ways I envied them. They had never known a time when Arabia had not been a major power. They came here as equals with everyone and were accepted cheerfully by the Nubians who treated them with the respect due to richer pilgrims and potential converts to the divine revelation of Islam.

Again in common with my generation, I was of a secular disposition and saw only damaging, enslaving darkness in any religion. We had even rejected the received wisdoms of Freud, Jung, Marx and their followers and embraced instead a political creed which had as its basis the eminent likelihood of ecological disaster and the slight possibility of an economic miracle. They called us the Anaemic Generation now: a decade or more that was out of step with the progress of history as it was presently interpreted. It suited me to know that I was an anachronism; it afforded me a special kind of security. Very few people took me seriously.

An Egyptian army officer marched past me as I crossed to the river-side of the corniche to look down at the half-completed stairways, the crumbling, poorly-mixed concrete and the piles of rat-infested rubble which the Korean engineers, who had put in the lowest tender for the work, had still neither repaired nor cleared. The officer glanced at me as if he recognised me but then went past, looking, with his neatly-trimmed moustache and rigid shoulders, the perfect image of a World War Two English Guards captain. Even his uniform was in the English style. I suppose Romans coming to 5th century Britain after some lapse of time would have been equally impressed to see a Celt striding through the streets of Londinium, impeccable in a slightly antiquated Centurion's kit. The whole casual story of the human race seemed to be represented in the town as I paused to look at the hulks of converted pleasure boats, home to swarms of Nubian families impoverished by the altered climate and the shift of tourism towards the Total Egypt Experience found in the comfort of Fort Sadat and New Memphis. Despite the piles of filthy garbage along the shore, Aswan had acquired the pleasant, nostalgic qualities of unfashionable British resorts like Morecombe or Yarmouth, a local population careless of most strangers save sometimes for the money they brought.

About halfway along the corniche I stopped at a little café and sat down on a cane chair, ordering mint tea from a proprietor whose ancient tarboosh might have escaped from the costume department of a touring production of *Death on the Nile.* He addressed me as "*effendi*" and his chosen brand of English seemed developed from old

British war movies. Like me, I thought, he was out of step with the times. When he brought the tea I told him to keep the change from a pound and again on the off-chance asked after my sister. I was surprised by the enthusiasm of his response. He knew the name von Bek and was approving when I told him of our relationship. "She is very good," he said. "A tip-top gentlewoman. But now, I think, she is unwell. It it hard to see the justice of it."

Pleased and a little alarmed, I asked if he knew where she lived.

"She lived in *Sharri al Sahahaldeen*, just off the *Sharri al Souk*." He pointed with his thumb back into town. "But that was more than a year ago. Oh, she is very well known here in Aswan. The poor people like her immensely. They call her *Saidneh Duukturah*."

"Doctor?" My sister had only rudimentary medical training. Her doctorate had been in archaeology. "She treats the sick?"

"Well, not so much any more. Now only if the hospitals refuse help. The Bisharim, in particular, love her. You know those nomads. They trust your sister only. But she moved from Sahahaldeen Street after some trouble. I heard she went to the English House over on the West Bank, but I'm not so sure. Perhaps you should ask the Bisharim." He raised his hand in welcome to a small man in a dark blue *gelabea* who walked briskly into the darkness of the shop's interior. "A customer." From his pocket he took a cut-throat razor. "*Naharak sa'id*," he called and, adopting the swagger of the expert barber, waved farewell to me and entered his shop.

"*Fi amani 'llah*." Picking up my hat I crossed to a rank where the usual two or three ill-used horses stood between the shafts of battered broughams, still the commonest form of taxi in Aswan. I approached the first driver, who stood flicking at flies with his ragged whip while he smoked a cigarette and chatted with his fellows. He wore an American sailor's hat, a faded T-shirt advertising some Russian artpopper, a pair of traditional baggy trousers exposing ulcerated calves and, on his feet, pink and black Roos. From the state of his legs I guess he had retained the habit, against all current warnings, of wading into the Nile to urinate. I asked him to take me first to the dam's administration office where, for courtesy's sake, I presented myself and made an appointment with my old aquaintance Georges Abidos, the Chief Press Officer, who had been called out to the northern end of the lake. His secretary said he was looking forward to seeing me tomorrow and handed me a welcoming note. I then asked the calash-driver if he knew the Bisharim camp on the outskirts of town. I had heard that in recent years the tribe had returned to its traditional sites. He was contemptuous. "Oh, yes, sir. The barbarians are still with us!" I told him I would give him another ten pounds to take me there and return. He made to bargain but then accepted, shrugging and gesturing for me to get in his carriage. I guessed he was maintaining some kind of face for himself. In my travels I had grown used to all kinds of mysterious body-language, frequently far harder to interpret than any spoken tongue.

We trotted back to town and jogged beside a river strewn with old plastic water-bottles, with all the miscellaneous filth from the boats that no legislation appeared able to limit, past flaking quasi-French facades still bearing the crests of Farouk and his ancestors and each now occupied by twenty or thirty families whose washing hung over the elaborate iron balconies and carved stone sphinxes like bunting celebrating some joyous national holiday. We passed convents and churches, mosques and graveyards, shanteys, monuments, little clumps of palm-trees sheltering donkeys and boys from a sun which as noon approached grew steadily more intense.

We went by the English holiday villas where hippies nowadays congregated; we passed the burned-out shells of warehouses and storerooms, victims of some forgotten riot, the stained walls sprayed with the emerald-coloured ankh of the Green Jihad, and eventually, turning inland again, reached the old Moslem necropolis, almost a mile long and half-a-mile across, surrounded by a low, mud wall and filled with every shape and size of stone or sarcophagus. Beyond this, further up the hill, I made out clumps of palms and the dark woollen tents of the Bisharim.

My driver reined in his horse some distance from the camp, beside a gate into the graveyard. "I will wait for you here," he said significantly.

2 : Ah, Whence, and Whither Flown Again, Who Knows?

The nomad camp, showing so few outward signs of Western influence, had the kind of self-contained dignity which city Arabs frequently manage to recreate in their homes and yet which is not immediately noticed by those visitors merely disgusted by, for instance, Cairo's squalor.

Sheikh Khamet ben Achmet was the patriarch of this particular clan. They had come in a month ago, he said, from the Sudan, to trade horses and camels. They all knew my sister but she had disappeared. He employed a slow, classical Arabic which was easy for me to understand and in which I could easily respond. "God has perhaps directed thy sister towards another vocation," he suggested gently. "It was only a short time since she would visit us whenever we put down our tents here. She had a particularly efficient cure for infections of the eye, but it was the women who went to her, chiefly." He looked at me with quiet amusement. "The best type of Englishwoman, as we say. Sometimes God sends us His beneficence in strange forms."

"Thou has no knowledge of her present dwelling?" I sipped the coffee a servant brought us. I was glad to be in the cool tent. Outside it was now at least 35°. There was little danger of freak rain today. He looked up at me from his ironic grey eyes. "No," he said. "She always visits us. When we needed her we would send messages to the Copt's house. You know, the carpenter who lives on the street leading from the great mosque to the souk."

I did not know him, I said.

"He is as gold-haired as thou. They nickname him The German, but I know he is a Copt from Alexandria. I think he is called Iskander. I know that he is easily found."

"Thou knowest my sister was an archaeologist?" I was a little hesitant.

"Indeed, I do! We discussed all manner of ancient things together and she had the courtesy to say that I was at least as informative as the great Egyptian Museum in Cairo!" He was amused by what he perceived as elegant flattery. My sister, if I still knew her, had done no more than to state her direct opinion.

It would have been ill-mannered of me to have left as soon as I had the information I sought, so I spent two further hours answering the Sheikh's questions about current American and European politics. I was not surprised that he was well-informed. I had seen his short-wave radio (doubtless full of *piles noires*) standing on the ivory-inlaid chest on the far side of the tent. I was also unsurprised by his interpretations of what he had learned. They were neither cynical nor unintelligent, but they were characteristic of certain desert Arabs who see everything in terms of power and opportunity and simply cannot grasp the reverence for political institutions we have in the West. For a few minutes I foolishly tried to re-educate him until it became clear I must give offence. Recalling my old rules, I accepted his terms. As a result we parted friends. Any Irish apologist for apartheid could not have been more approving of my good manners.

When I got up to leave, the old man took my arm and wished me God's grace and help in finding my sister. "She was associated with Jews." He spoke significantly. "Those who did not like her said that she was a witch. And it is true that two of my women saw her consorting with the spell-seller from the Souk. The one called Lallah Zenobia. The black woman. Thou and I art men of the world and understand that it is superstitious folly. But thou knowest how women are. And they are often," he added in an even lower tone, "susceptible to Yehudim flattery and lies."

It was by no means the first time I had to accept such sentiments from the mouth of one who was otherwise hospitality, tolerance and kindness personified. To persuade a desert Arab that Jews are not in direct and regular touch with Satan and all His minions is still no easier than persuading a Dixie Baptist that the doors of a Catholic Church are not necessarily a direct gateway to Hell. One is dealing with powerful survival myths which only direct experience will disprove. In such circumstances I never mention my mother's family. I said I would visit Iskander the Carpenter. At this point a braying, bellowing and snorting chorus grew so loud I could barely hear his elaborate goodbyes. The stock was being beaten back from the water. As I emerged from the tent I saw my driver in the distance. He was sitting on the wall of the cemetery feinting with his whip at the boys and girls who flowed like a tide around him, daring one another to run within his range.

3 : *Crystal to the Wizard Eye*

I had no difficulty in discovering Iskander the Carpenter. He was a slight man wearing a pair of faded denim overalls. Sanding off a barley-sugar chairleg, he sat just inside his workshop, which was open to the street and displayed an entire suite of baroque bedroom and living room furniture he had almost completed. He chose to speak in French. "It is for a couple getting married this weekend. At least they are spending their money on furniture rather than the wedding itself!" He put down his chairleg and shook my hand. He was fair-skinned and blond, as Sheikh Achmet had said, though I could not have taken him for anything but Egyptian. His features could have come straight from the Egyptian Museum's clay statue displays of ancient tradespeople. He might have been a foreman on a Middle Kingdom site. He turned up a chair which still had to have the upholstery over its horsehair seat, indicated that I should sit and sent his son to get us a couple of bottles of Pyramid beer.

"Of course I know Saidneh Duukturah. She was my friend. That one," he pointed to his disappearing boy, "owes his life to her. He was poisoned. She treated him. He is well. It is true I knew where she lived and would get messages to her. But for a year or more she went away from us. Until recently she was staying at the English House. There are many rumours. Most of them are simply stupid. She is no witch. She was a woman blessed by God with the healing touch. The other woman, now, is undoubtably a witch. My wife heard that your sister fell in love and went to the Somalin, Zenobia, for a philtre. Certainly, by chance, my wife saw her handing Zenobia a heavy purse. A Cairene purse, she was sure."

"I do not know what that is." I moved further into the shade. Outside, Aswan had fallen into a doze as the population closed its shutters until mid-afternoon. The yellow walls of the houses were now almost blistering to the touch.

"A purse of money, that's all. It used to mean a bag of gold. About twenty sovereigns. That is what a witch demands for a very powerful spell. Something very valuable, my friend."

"My sister was buying a charm from a spell-seller?"

"A powerful one, yes. That negress has been involved with the police more than once. She was suspected of killing a rival suitor at the behest of another, of being responsible for the death of a man who was owed over a thousand pounds by another man. Now, if your sister was disposed to witchcraft, why would she go to a witch and pay her a healthy sum for a job she could as readily do herself?"

I agreed it was unlikely my sister was a witch. I asked how the matter had come to official attention.

"The police went to see her, I think. My wife's friend—friend no more—gossiped. They arrested Zenobia, then let your sister go. You should visit the *mamur* at the *markaz*, the police department. The *mamur* here is a very just man. He never accepts money unless he can do whatever it is he promises. His name is Inspector el-Bayoumi. If anyone knows where your sister is living in Aswan he probably will."

By the time I had discussed the affairs of the day and thanked the carpenter for the beer, it was already cooler and I walked down to the *Sharri el Souk* which was beginning to open for business again, filling with women in black lacy *milayum* which barely revealed the vivid colours of their house dresses beneath, clutching bright plastic shopping bags and going about their weekend buying. Because it was Friday afternoon the butchers were displaying their calves' heads and bullock tails, their sheep's hearts and heads, their divided carcasses, all protected from an unforgiving sun by the thick coating of black flies which also covered the fish and offal on other stalls. Sellers of turkeys, pigeons and chickens took water in their mouths to force between the beaks of their wares so that they would not dehydrate before they were sold, and seemed to be kissing, tenderly, each one. Cheerful greengrocers called out the virtues of their squash, mangoes, potatoes or green beans. Gas lorries, electroscoots, bicycles and a few official cars moved in slow competition with rickshaws, donkeys, mules or camels through alleys where, every so often, a bright sign would advertise in English the virtues of unobtainable Panasonic televisions or Braun refrigerators and others would, almost pathetically, alert the passerby to the Color Xerox machine or Your Local Fax Office. Like every similar souk in the Arab world, the tools and artefacts of the centuries were crowded side by side and functioning in perfect compatability. Aswan had adapted, far more readily and more cheerfully, to modern energy restraints than had London, for instance, where it had taken an Act of Parliament to reintroduce the public horse trough.

I made my way to the northern end of the street where the police station, the *markaz*, resembling an old British garrison, was guarded by two boys in serge khaki who were armed with the Lee Enfield 303s with which Lawrence had armed his men for the Desert War and which had, then, been an Arab's prized possession. Now it was unlikely any reliable ammunition existed for these antiques. I understood only the crack militia was allowed to sport the old Kalashnikovs or M16s issued to regular infantry. With the end of international arms trading, almost any well-made gun was valuable, if only as status.

I had no appointment and was informed by the bright young civilian woman on the duty desk that Inspector el-Bayoumi would be back from New Town, the concrete development near the airport, in about an hour. I gave my name, my business, and said I would be back at about five-thirty. Courteously she assured me that the Inspector would await me.

4 : Her Heart All Ears and Eyes, Lips Catching the Avalanche Of the Golden Ghost

I had forgotten how much time one had to spend on enquiries of this kind. I returned to my apartment to find an envelope pushed under my door. It was not, as I had hoped, from my sister, but a letter welcoming me to Aswan, a short personal note from my friend Georges, a list of appointments with various engineers and officials, some misleading publicity about the dam, consisting mainly of impressive photographs, a variety of press releases stressing the plans for "an even better dam" and so on. I went out again having glanced at them. I was obsessed with all the mysteries with which I had been presented in a single day. How had my sister metamorphosed from a dedicated archaeologist to some kind of local Mother Theresa?

Disturbed by my own speculations I forced myself to think about the next day's work when I would be discussing methods of reducing pollution in all its varieties and rebuilding the dam to allow silt down to the arable areas. The signs of serious "redesertisation", as ugly official jargon termed it, were now found everywhere in the Nile valley. In other words, the Aswan Dam was now seriously contributing to ecological damage as well as helping to wipe out our most important links with the remote past. I could not believe how intelligent scientists, who were not those industrial developers motivated only by greed, failed to accept the dreadful psychic damage being done to people whose whole identities were bound up with a particular and very specific landscape. My own identity, for instance, was profoundly linked to a small Oxfordshire village which had remained unchanged for hundreds of years after successfully resisting developers wanting to surround it with high quality modern properties instead of its existing beeches and oaks.

Few Egyptians were in such comfortable circumstances or could make any choice but the one promising the most immediate benefit, yet they had the same understanding of their tribal homes and what values they represented, and still resisted all attempts to force them to lose their traditional clothes, language and attitudes and make them modern citizens of their semi-democratic society. Unfortunately, this attitude also extended to a dam now much older than many of its staff and never at any time an engineering miracle. UNEC had plans for a replacement. Currently they and the Rajhidi government were arguing over the amounts each would contribute. Happily, that was not my problem.

With a slightly clearer head, I walked to the Post Office on the corner of Abdel el Taheer street. Though almost fifty years had passed since the First Revolution, the building still bore the outlines of earlier royal insignia. The elaborate cast-ironwork on doors and windows was of that "Oriental" pattern exported from the foundries of Birmingham to adorn official buildings throughout the Empire east of Gibraltar. Even by the 1970s the stuff was still available from stock, during the brief period after the death of Britain's imperial age and before the birth of that now much-despised and admittedly reckless Thatcher period known ironically as "the Second Empire", the period which had shaped my own expectations of life as well as those of uncounted millions of my fellows, the period in which my uncle had died, a soldier in the Falklands cause.

I entered the main door's cool archway and walked through dusty shafts of light to a tiled counter where I asked to speak to the Post Master. After a moment's wait I was shown into his little gloomy mahogany office, its massive fan constantly stirring piles of documents which moved like a perpetually unsettled flight of doves. A small, handsome Arab entered and closed the door carefully behind him. His neat, Abraham Lincoln beard suggested religious devotion. I told him that my name was von Bek and I was expecting mail. I handed him an envelope I had already prepared. On the outside was my name and occupation. Inside was the conventional "purse"—actually another envelope containing a few pounds. I said I would appreciate his personal interest in my mail and hoped he could ensure it was available to me the moment it arrived. Absently, he took the envelope and put it in his trouser pocket. He had brightened at the sound of my name. "Are you related to that woman of virtue whom we know here in Aswan?" He spoke measured, cultured Arabic with the soft accents of Upper Egypt.

"My sister." I was trying to locate her, I said. Perhaps her mail was delivered here?

"It has not been collected, Si von Bek, for several months. Yet she has been seen in Aswan recently. There was a small scandal. I understand that El Haj Sheikh Ibrahim Abu Halil intervened. Have you asked him about your sister?"

"Is he the governor?"

He laughed. Clearly the idea of the governor intervening on

behalf of an ordinary member of the public amused him. "No. Sheikh Abu Halil is the gentleman so many come to Aswan to see these days. He is the great Sufi now. We are blessed in this. God sends us everything that is good, even the rain. So much more grows and blooms. People journey to us from all over the world. Here, God has chosen to reveal a glimpse of Paradise."

I was impressed by his optimism. I told him I would go to see Sheikh Abu Halil as soon as possible. Meanwhile I had an appointment with the police chief. At this his face grew a little uncertain, but his only response was some conventional greeting concerning Allah's good offices.

Police Inspector el-Bayoumi was one of those suave career officers produced by the new academies. His manners were perfect, his hospitality generous and discreet, and when I had replied to his question, telling him where I had been born in England, he confessed affectionate familiarity with another nearby Cotswold village. Together, we deplored the damage tourism had done to the environment and confessed it to be a major problem in both our countries, which depended considerably on the very visitors who contributed to the erosion. He sighed. "I think the human race has rather foolishly cancelled many of its options."

Since he preferred to speak it, I replied in English. "Perhaps our imaginative resources are becoming as scarce as our physical ones?"

"There has been a kind of psychic withering," he agreed. "And its worst symptom, in my view, Mr. von Bek, is found in the religious and political fundamentalism to which so many subscribe. As if, by some sort of sympathetic magic, the old, simpler days will return. We live in complicated times with complicated problems. It's a sad fact that they require sophisticated solutions."

I admitted I had been schooled in many of those fundamentalist notions and sometimes found them difficult to resist. We chatted about this for a while. Coffee was brought, together with a selection of delicious *gurrahiya* pastries, whose secret the Egyptians inherited from the Turks, and we talked for another half-hour, during which time we took each other's measure and agreed the world would be a better place if civilised people like ourselves were allowed a greater voice. Whereupon, in that sometimes abrupt change of tone Arabs have, which can mislead Europeans into thinking they have somehow given offence, Inspector el-Bayoumi asked what he could do for me.

"I'm looking for my sister. She's an economic archaeologist who came here two and a half years ago with the Burbank College Project. It was an international team. Only about half were from California and those returned the next year, after the big earthquake. Most of them, of course, had lost relatives. My sister stayed on with the remaining members." I did not mention her talk of a wonderful discovery out in the Western Sahara. Their sonavids had picked up a New Kingdom temple complex almost perfectly preserved but buried some hundred feet under the sand. My sister had been very excited about it. It was at least on a par with the discovery of the Tutankhamen treasures and probably of far greater historical importance. She and the team kept the discovery quiet, of course, especially since so many known monuments had suffered. Naturally, there were some conflicts of interest. There was little she could tell me in a letter and most of that was a bit vague, making reference to personal or childhood incidents whose relevance escaped me. I added delicately. "You know about the discovery, naturally."

He smiled as he shook his handsome head. "No, Mr. von Bek, I don't. I think an elaborate dig would not escape my notice." He paused, asking me if he might smoke. I told him I was allergic to cigarette smoke and he put his case away. Regretfully, he said: "I should tell you that your sister is a little disturbed. She was arrested by us about a year ago. There was something we had to follow up. An outbreak of black magic amongst the local people. We don't take such things very seriously until it's possible to detect a cult growing. Then we have to move to break it up as best we can. Such things are not a serious problem in London, but for a policeman in Aswan they are fairly important. We arrested a known witch, a Somali woman they call Madame Zenobia, and with her an Englishwoman, also rumoured to be practising. That was your sister, Mr. von Bek. She was deranged and had to be given a sedative. Eventually, we decided against charging her and released her into the custody of Lady Roper."

"The Consul's wife?"

"He's the Honorary Consul here in Aswan now. They have a large house on the West Bank, not far from the Ali Khan's tomb. You can't see it from this side. It is our miracle. Locally, it's called the English House. More recently they've called it the Rose House. You'll find no mysteries there!"

"That's where my sister's staying?"

"No longer. She left Aswan for a while. When she came back she joined the community around Sheikh Abu Halil and I understand her to be living in the old holiday villas on the Edfu road, near the race course. I'll gladly put a man to work on the matter. We tend not to pursue people too much in Aswan. Your sister is a good woman. An honest woman. I hope she has recovered herself."

Thanking him I said I hoped my search would not involve the time of a hardworking police officer. I got up to leave. "And what happened to Madame Zenobia?"

"Oh, the courts were pretty lenient. She got a year, doing quarry work for the Restoration Department in Cairo. She was a fit woman. She'll be even fitter now. Hard labour is a wonderful cure for neurosis! And far more socially useful that concocting love potions or aborting cattle."

He sounded like my old headmaster. As an afterthought, I said, "I gather Sheikh Abu Halil took an interest in my sister's case."

He flashed me a look of intelligent humour. "Yes, he did. He is much respected here. Your sister is a healer. The Sufi is a healer. He sometimes makes an accurate prophecy. He has a following all over the world, I believe."

I appreciated his attempt at a neutral tone, given his evident distaste for matters psychic and mystical. We shared, I think, a similar outlook.

I found myself asking him another question. "What was the evidence against my sister, Inspector?"

He had hoped I would not raise the matter, but was prepared for it. "Well," he began slowly, "for instance, we had a witness who saw her passing a large bag of money to the woman. The assumption was that she was paying for a spell. A powerful one. A love philtre, possibly, but it was also said that she wanted a man dead. He was the only other member of her team who had remained behind. There was some suggestion, Mr. von Bek," he paused again, "that he made her pregnant. But this was all the wildest gossip. He did in fact die of a heart attack shortly after the reported incident. Sometimes we must treat such cases as murder. But we only had circumstantial evidence. The man was a drug addict and apparently had tried to force your sister to give him money. There was just a hint of blackmail involved in the case, you see. These are all, of course, the interpretations of a policeman. Maybe the man had been an ex-lover, no more. Maybe she wanted him to love her again?"

"It wasn't Noone, was it?"

"It was not her estranged husband. He is, I believe, still in New Zealand."

"You really think she got tangled up in black magic?"

"When confused, men turn to war and women to magic. She was not, as the Marrakshim say, with the caravan." He was just a little sardonic now. "But she was adamant that she did not wish to go home."

"What did she tell you?"

"She denied employing the witch. She claimed the Somali woman was her only friend. Otherwise she said little. But her manner was all the time distracted, as if she imagined herself to be surrounded by invisible witnesses. We were not unsympathetic. The psychiatrist from the German hospital came to see her. Your sister is a saintly woman who helped the poor and the sick and asked for no reward. She enriched us. We were trying to help her, you know."

He had lost his insouciance altogether now and spoke with controlled passion. "It could be that your sister had an ordinary breakdown. Too much excitement in her work, too much sun. Caring too much for the hardships of others. She tried to cure the whole town's ills and that task is impossible for any individual. Her burden was too heavy. You could see it written in every line of her face, every movement of her body. We wanted her to recover. Some suspected she was in the witch's power, but in my own view she carried a personal weight of guilt, perhaps. Probably pointlessly, too. You know how woman are. They are kinder, more feeling creatures than men."

5 : The Seasons of Home— Aye, Now They Are Remembered!

That evening, while there was still light, I took the felucca across the Nile, to the West Bank. The ferryman, clambering down from his high mast where he had been reefing his sail, directed me through the village to a dirt road winding up the hillside a hundred yards or so from the almost austere resting place of the Ali Khan. "You will see it," he assured me. "But get a boy."

There were a couple of dozen children waiting for me on the quay. I selected a bright looking lad of about ten. He wore a ragged Japanese T-shirt with the inscription I LOVE SEX WAX, a pair of cut-off jeans and Adidas trainers. In spite of the firmness with which I singled him out, we were followed by the rest of the children all the way to the edge of the village. I had a couple of packs of old electronic watches which I distributed, to a pantomime of disappointment from the older children. Watches had ceased to be fashionable currency since I had last been in Aswan. Now, from their requests, I learned it was "real" fountain pens. They showed me a couple of Sheaffers some tourist had already exchanged for their services as guides and companions of the road.

I had no fountain pen for the boy who took me to the top of the hill and pointed down into the little valley where, amongst the sand and the rocks, had been erected a large two-storey house, as solidly Edwardian as any early twentieth century vicarage. Astonishingly, it was planted with cedars, firs and other hardy trees shading a garden to rival anything I had ever seen in Oxfordshire. There were dozens of varieties of roses, of every possible shade, as well as hollyhocks, snapdragons, foxgloves, marigolds and all the flowers one might find in an English July garden. A peculiar wall about a metre high surrounded the entire mirage and I guessed that it disguised some kind of extraordinarily expensive watering and sheltering apparatus which had allowed the owners to do the impossible and bring a little bit of rural England to Upper Egypt. The grounds covered several acres. I saw some stables, a garage, and a woman on the front lawn. She was seated in a faded deckchair watching a fiche-reader or a video which she rested in her left hand. With her right hand she took a glorious drink from the little table beside her and sipped through the straw. As I drew nearer, my vision was obscured by the trees and the wall, but I guessed she was about sixty-five, dressed in a thoroughly unfashionable Marks and Ashley smock, a man's trilby hat and a pair of rubber-tyre sandals. She looked up as I reached the gate and called "Good afternoon". Happy with cash, my boy departed.

"Lady Roper?"

She had a quick, intelligent, swarthy face, her curls all grey beneath the hat, her long hands expressive even when still. "I'm Diana Roper."

"My name's Paul von Bek. I'm Beatrice's brother."

"The engineer!" She was full of welcome. "My goodness, you know, I think Bea could foretell the future. She *said* you'd be turning up here about now."

"I wrote and told her!" I was laughing as the woman unlocked the gate and let me in. "I knew about this job months ago."

"You're here on business."

"I'm going through the rituals of sorting out a better dam and trying to do something about the climactic changes. I got sent because I know a couple of people here—and because I asked to come. But there's little real point to my being here."

"You don't sound very hopeful, Mr. von Bek." She led me towards the back of the house, to a white wrought-iron conservatory which was a relatively recent addition to the place and must have been erected by some forgotten imperial dignitary of the last century.

"I'm always hopeful that people will see reason, Lady Roper."

We went into the sweet-smelling ante-room, whose glass had been treated so that it could admit only a certain amount of light, or indeed reflect all the light to perform some needed function elsewhere. Despite its ancient appearance, I guessed the house to be using up-to-date EE technologies and to be completely self-sufficient. "What an extraordinary garden," I said.

"Imported Kent clay." She offered me a white basket chair. "With a fair bit of Kenyan topsoil, I understand. We didn't have it done. We got it all dirt cheap. It takes such a long time to travel anywhere these days, most people don't want the place. It belonged to one of the Fayeds, before they all went off to Malaysia. But have you looked carefully at our roses, Mr. von Bek? They have a sad air to them, a sense of someone departed, someone mourned. Each bush was planted for a dead relative, they say." Her voice grew distant. "Of course, the new rain has helped enormously. I've survived because I know the rules. Women frequently find their intuition very useful in times of social unrest. But things are better now, aren't they? We simply refuse to learn. We refuse to learn."

Grinning as if enjoying a game, a Nubian girl of about sixteen brought us a tray of English cakes and a pot of Assam tea. I wondered how I had lost the thread of Lady Roper's conversation.

"We do our best," I said, letting the girl take tongs to an éclair and with a flourish pop it on my plate. "I believe Bea lived here for a while."

"My husband took quite a fancy to her. As did I. She was a sweetie. And so bright. Is that a family trait? Yes, we shared a great deal. It was a luxury for me, you know, to have such company. Not many people have been privileged as she and I were privileged." She nodded with gentle mystery, her eyes in the past. "We were friends of your uncle. That was the funny thing we found out. All at Cambridge together in the late sixties. We thought conservation an important subject *then.* What? Fifty years ago, almost? Such a jolly boy. He joined up for extremely complicated reasons, we felt. Did you know why?"

I had never really wondered. My picture of my mother's brother was of the kind of person who would decide on a military career, but evidently they had not been acquainted with that man at all. Finding this disturbing, I attempted to return to my subject. "I was too young to remember him. My sister was more curious than I. Did she seem neurotic to you, while she was here?"

"On the contrary. She was the sanest of us all! Sound as a bell upstairs, as Bernie always said. Sharp intelligence. But, of course, she had been there, you see. And could confirm everything we had been able to piece together at this end."

"You're referring to the site they discovered?"

"That, of course, was crucial. Especially at the early stages. Yes, the site was extraordinary. We went out to see it with her, Bernie and I. What a mind-blower, Paul! Amazing experience. Even the small portion they had excavated. Four mechanical sifters just sucking the sand gradually away. It would have taken years in the old days. Unfortunately three of the operators left after the earthquake and the sifters were recalled for some crucial rescue work over in Sinai. And then, of course, everything changed."

"I'm not sure I'm..."

"After the ship came and took Bea."

"A ship? On the Nile?"

She frowned at me for a moment and then her tone changed to one of distant friendliness. "You'll probably want a word with Bernie. You'll find him in his playroom. Nadja will take you. And I'm here if you need to know anything."

She glanced away, through the glass walls of the conservatory and was at once lost in melancholy reflection of the roses and their guardian trees.

6 : The Smoke Along the Track

A tape of some antique radio programme was playing as I knocked on the oak door and was admitted by a white-haired old man wearing a pair of overalls and a check shirt, with carpet slippers on his feet. His skin had the healthy sheen of a sun-baked reptile and his blue eyes were brilliant with trust. I was shocked enough to remain where I was, even as he beckoned me in. He turned down his stereo, a replica of some even older audio contraption, and stood proudly to display a room full of books and toys. One wall was lined with glass shelves on which miniature armies battled amidst a wealth of tiny trees and buildings. "You don't look much like a potential playmate!" His eyes strayed towards the brilliant jackets of his books.

"And you're not entirely convincing as Mr. Dick, sir." I stood near the books, which were all well-ordered, and admired his illustrated Dickens. The temperature in the room was, I guessed, thoroughly controlled. Should the power fail for just a few hours the desert would fade and modify this room as if it had been a photograph left for an hour in the sun.

My retort seemed to please him. He grinned and came forward. "I'm Bernie Roper. While I have no immediate enemies, I enjoy in this room the bliss of endless childhood. I have my lead soldiers, my bears and rabbits, my model farm, and I read widely. *Treasure Island* is very good, as are the 'William' books, and Edgar Rice Burroughs and, as you say, Charles Dickens, though he's a bit on the scarey side sometimes. E. Nesbit and H.G. Wells and Shaw. I enjoy so much. For music I have the very best of *Children's Favourites* from the BBC—a mixture of comic songs, Gilbert and Sullivan, *Puff the Magic Dragon*, *The Laughing Policeman*, popular classics and light opera. Flanders and Swann, Danny Kaye, *Sparky's Magic Piano*, *Peter and the Wolf* and *Song of the South*. Do you know any of those? But I'm a silly chap! You're far too young. They'd even scrapped *Children's Hour* before you were born. Oh, dear. Never to enjoy *Larry the Lamb* or Norman and Henry Bones, the Boy Detectives! Oh!" he exclaimed with a knowing grin, "Calamity!" Then he returned his attention to his toys for a moment. "You think I should carry more responsibility?"

"No." I had always admired him as a diplomat. He deserved the kind of retirement that suited him.

"I feel sorry for the children," he said. "The pleasures of childhood are denied to more and more of them as their numbers increase. Rajhid and Abu Halil are no real solution, are they? We who remember the Revolution had hoped to have turned the desert green by now. I plan to die here, Mr.—?"

"My name's von Bek. I'm Bea's brother."

"My boy! Thank goodness I offered an explanation. I'm not nearly as eccentric as I look! 'Because I could not stop for Death, He kindly stopped for me. We shared a carriage, just we two, and Immortality.' Emily Dickinson, I believe. But I could also be misremembering. 'The child is Father to the Man,' you know. And the lost childhood of

Judas. Did you read all those poems at school?"

"I was probably too young again," I said. "We didn't do poetry as such."

"I'm so sorry. All computer studies nowadays, I suppose."

"Not all, sir." The old fashioned courtesy surprised us both. Sir Bernard acted as one cheated and I almost apologised. Yet it was probably the first time I had used the form of address without irony. I had, I realised, wanted to show respect. Sir Bernard had come to the same understanding. "Oh, well. You're a kind boy. But you'll forgive me, I hope, if I return to my preferred world."

"I'm looking for my sister, Sir Bernard. Actually, I'm pretty worried about her."

Without irritation, he sighed. "She was a sweet woman. It was terrible. And nobody believing her."

"Believing what, Sir Bernard?"

"About the spaceship, you know. But that's Di's field, really. Not my area of enthusiasm at all. I like to make time stand still. We each have a different way of dealing with the fact of our own mortality, don't we?" He strolled to one of his displays and picked up a charging 17th Lancer. "Into the Valley of Death rode the six hundred."

"Thank you for seeing me, Sir Bernard."

"Not at all, Paul. She talked about you. I liked her. I think you'll find her either attending Abu Halil's peculiar gymnasium or at the holiday homes. Where those Kenyan girls and boys are now living."

"Thank you. Goodbye, sir."

"Bye, bye!" Humming some stirring air, the former Director General of the United Nations hovered, contented, over his miniature Death or Glory Boys.

7 : Another Relay in the Chain of Fire

Lady Roper had remained in her conservatory. She rose as I

entered. "Was Bernie able to help?"

"I could be narrowing things down." I was anxious to get back to the East Bank before dark. "Thank you for your kindness. I tried to find a phone number for you."

"We're not on the phone, lovie. We don't need one."

"Sir Bernard mentioned a spaceship." I was not looking forward to her reply.

"Oh, dear, yes," she said "The flying saucer people. I think one day they will bring us peace, don't you? I mean one way or another. This is better than death for me, at any rate, Paul. But perhaps they have a purpose for us. Perhaps an unpleasant one. I don't think anybody would rule that out. What could we do if that were the case? Introduce a spy? That has not proved a successful strategy. We know that much, sadly. It's as if all that's left of Time is here. A few shreds from a few ages."

Again I was completely nonplussed and said nothing.

"I think you share Sir B's streak of pessimism. Or realism is it?"

"Well, we're rather different, actually…" I began to feel foolish.

"He was happier as Ambassador, you know. Before the UN. And then we were both content to retire here. We'd always loved it. The Fayeds had us out here lots of times, for those odd parties. We were much younger. You probably think we're both barking mad." When I produced an awkward reply she was sympathetic. "There *is* something happening here. It's a *centre.* You can feel it everywhere. It's an ideal place. Possibly we shall be the ones left to witness the birth of the New Age."

At that moment all I wished to do was save my sister from that atmosphere of half-baked mysticism and desperate faith, to get her back to the relative reality of London and a doctor who would know what was wrong with her and be able to treat it.

"Bea was never happier than when she was in Aswan, you know," said Lady Roper.

"She wrote and told me as much."

"Perhaps she risked a bit more than was wise. We all admire her for it. What I don't understand is why she was so thick with Lallah Zenobia. The woman's psychic, of course, but very unsophisticated."

"You heard about the witness? About the purse?"

"Naturally."

"And you, too, are sure it was a purse?"

"I suppose so. It's Cairo slang, isn't it, for a lot of money? The way the Greeks always say 'seven years' when they mean a long time has passed. Bernie's actually ill, you realise? He's coherent much of the time. A form of P.D. we were told. From the water when we were in Washington. He's determined to make the best of it. He's sweet, isn't he?"

"He's an impressive man. You don't miss England?"

She offered me her hand. "Not a bit. You're always welcome to stay if you are bored over there. Or the carping materialism of the Old Country gets to you. Simplicity's the keynote at the Rose House. Bernie says the British have been sulking for years, like the Lost Boys deprived of their right to go a-hunting and a-pirating at will. I'm afraid, Paul, that we don't think very much of home any more."

8 : And All These in Their Helpless Days...

The great Egyptian sun was dropping away to the horizon as in the company of some forty blue-cowled Islamic schoolgirls and a bird-catcher, I sailed back to the East. Reflected in the Nile the sky was the colour of blood and saffron against every tone of dusty blue; the rocks, houses and palms dark violet silhouettes, sparkling here and there as lamps were lit, signalling the start of Aswan's somewhat orderly nightlife. Near the landing stage I ate some *mulakhiya*, rice and an antique salad at Mahommeds' Cafetria, drank some mint tea and went back to the Osiris, half expecting to find that my sister had left word, but the Hindu woman had no messages and handed me my key with a quick smile of encouragement.

I slept poorly, kept awake by the constant cracking of a chemical "equaliser" in the basement and the creak of the all-but-useless wind-generator on the roof. It was ironic that Aswan, so close to the source of enormous quantities of electricity, was as cruelly rationed as everyone.

I refused to believe that my sister, who was as sane as I was and twice as intelligent, had become entangled with a black magic flying saucer cult. Her only purpose for associating with such people would be curiosity, perhaps in pursuit of some anthropological research connected with her work. I was, however, puzzled by her secrecy. Clearly, she was deliberately hiding her whereabouts. I hoped that, when I returned the next day, I would know where she was.

My meetings were predictably amiable and inconsequential. I had arrived a little late, having failed to anticipate the levels of security at the dam. There were police, militia and security people everywhere, both on the dam itself and in all the offices and operations areas. I had to show my pass to eleven different people. The dam was under increased threat from at least three different organisations, the chief being Green Jihad. Our main meetings were held in a large, glass-walled room overlooking the lake. I was glad to meet so many staff, though we all knew that any decisions about the dam would not be made by us but by whomever triumphed in the Geneva negotiations. It was also good to discover that earlier attitudes towards the dam were changing slightly and new thinking was being done. Breakfasted and lunched, I next found myself guest of honor at a full-scale Egyptian dinner which must have taken everyone's rations for a month, involved several entertainments and lastly a good deal of noisy toasting, in cokes and grape juice, our various unadmired leaders.

The Cairene Purse

MICHAEL MOORCOCK

At the Hotel Osiris, when I got back that night, there was no note for me so I decided next day to visit the old vacation villas before lunching as arranged at the Cataract with Georges Abidos, who had told me that he was retiring as Public Relations officer for the dam. I had a hunch that my sister was probably living with the neo-hippies. The following morning I ordered a calash to pick me up and sat on the board beside the skinny, cheerful driver as his equally thin horse picked her way slowly through busy Saturday streets until we were on the long, cracked concrete road with the railway yards on one side and the river on the other, flanked by dusty palms, which led past the five-storey Moorish-style vacation complex, a tumble of typical tourist architecture of the kind once found all around the Mediterranean, Adriatic and parts of the Black and Red Seas. The white stucco was patchy and the turquoise trim on window-frames and doors was peeling, but the new inhabitants, who had occupied it when the Swedish owners finally abandoned it, had put their stamp on it. Originally the place had been designed for Club Med, but had never sustained the required turnover, even with its special energy dispensations, and had been sold several times over the past ten years. Now garishly-dressed young squatters from the wealthy African countries, from the Australias, North and South America, as well as Europe and the Far East, had covered the old complex with their sometimes impressive murals and decorative graffiti. I read a variety of slogans. LET THE BLOOD CONSUME THE FIRE, said one. THE TYGERS OF THE MIND RULE THE JUNGLE OF THE HEART, said another. I had no relish for such undisciplined nonsense and did not look forward to meeting the occupants of this bizarre New New Age fortress. Psychedelia, even in its historical context, had never attracted me.

As I dismounted from the calash I was greeted by a young woman energetically cleaning the old Club Med brass plate at the gate. She had those startling green eyes in a dark olive skin which one frequently comes across everywhere in Egypt and are commonly believed to be another inheritance from the Pharoanic past. Her reddish hair was braided with multi-coloured ribbons and she wore a long green silk smock which complemented her eyes.

"Hi!" Her manner was promiscuously friendly. "I'm Lips. Which is short for Eclipse, to answer your question. Don't get the wrong idea. You're here to find a relative, right?" Her accent was Canadian with a trace of something else, possibly Ukrainian. "What's your name?"

"Paul," I said. "My sister's called Bea. Are the only people who visit you trying to find relatives?"

"I just made an assumption from the way you look. I'm pretty good at sussing people out." Then she made a noise of approving excitement. "Becky Beak, is it? She's famous here. She's a healer and an oracle. She's special."

"Could you take me to her apartment?" I did my best not to show impatience with the girl's nonsense.

"Lips" answered me with a baffled smile. "No. I mean, sure I could take you to one of her rooms. But she's not here now."

"Do you know where she went?"

The girl was vaguely apologetic. "Mercury? Wherever the ship goes."

My irritation grew more intense. But I controlled myself. "You've no idea when the ship gets back?"

"Now? Yesterday? There's so much time-bending involved. No. You just have to hope."

I walked past her into the complex.

9 : Fast Closing Toward The Undelighted Night...

By the time I had spoken to a dozen or so *enfants des fleurs* I had found myself a guide who introduced himself as Magic Mungo and wore brilliant face-paint beneath his straw hat. He had on an old pair of glitterjeans which whispered and flashed as he walked. His jacket announced in calligraphic Arabic phonetic English: THE NAME IS THE GAME. He was probably no older than thirteen. He asked me what I did and when I told him he said he, too, planned to become an engineer "and bring back the power." This amused me and restored my temper. "And what will you do about the weather?" I asked.

"It's not the weather," he told me, "not Nature—it's the ships. And it's not the dam, or the lake, that's causing the storms and stuff. It's the Reens."

I misheard him. I thought he was blaming the Greens. Then I realised, belatedly, that he was expressing a popular notion amongst the New New Agers, which by the time I had heard it several times more had actually begun to improve my mood. The Reens, the flying saucer people, were used by the hippies as an explanation for everything they couldn't understand. In rejecting Science, they had substituted only a banal myth. Essentially, I was being told that the Gods had taken my sister. In other words they did not know where she was. At last, after several further short but keen conversations, in various rug-strewn galleries and cushion-heavy chambers smelling strongly of kif, incense and patchouli, I met a somewhat older woman, with gray streaks in her long black hair and a face the colour and texture of well-preserved leather.

"This is Ayesha." Mungo gulped comically. "She-who-must-be-obeyed!" He ran to the woman who smiled a perfectly ordinary smile as she embraced him. "We encourage their imaginations," she said. "They read books here and everything. Are you looking for Beck?"

Warily expecting more Reen talk, I admitted that I was trying to find my sister.

"She went back to Aswan. I think she was at the medrassah for a bit—you know, with the Sufi—but after that she returned to town. If she's not there, she's in the desert again. She goes there to meditate,

I'm told. If she's not there, she's not anywhere. Around here, I mean."

I was relieved by the straightforward nature of her answer. "I'm greatly obliged. I thought you, too, were going to tell me she was taken into space by aliens!"

Ayesha joined in my amusement. "Oh, no, of course not. That was more than a year ago!"

10 : Thoughts of Too Old a Colour Nurse My Brain

I decided to have a note delivered to the Sufi, El Haj Ibrahim Abu Halil, telling him that I planned to visit him next day, then, with a little time to spare before my appointment, I strolled up the corniche, past the boat-ghetto at the upper end, and along the more fashionable stretches where some sporadic attempt was made to give the railings fresh coats of white paint and where a kiosk, closed since my first time here, advertised in bleached Latin type the *Daily Telegraph, Le Monde* and the *New York Herald-Tribune.* A few thin strands of white smoke rose from the villages on Elephantine Island, and from *Gazirat-al-Bustan,* Plantation Island, whose bontanical gardens, begun by Lord Kitchener, had long since mutated into marvellously exotic jungle, came the laughter of the children and teenagers who habitually spent their free days there.

Outside the kiosk stood an old man holding a bunch of faded and ragged international newspapers under one arm and *El Misr* under the other. "All today!" he called vigorously in English, much as a London coster shouted "All fresh!" A professional cry rather than any sort of promise. I bought an *El Misr,* only a day old, and glanced at the headlines as I walked up to the park. There seemed nothing unusually alarming in the paper. Even the EC rate had not risen in the last month. As I tried to open the sheet a gust came off the river and the yellow-grey paper began to shred in my hands. It was low-density recyke, unbulked by the sophisticated methods of the West. Before I gave up and dumped the crumpled mess into the nearest reclamation bin I had glimpsed references to the UNEC conference in Madagascar and something about examples of mass hysteria in Old Paris and Bombay, where a group called *Reincarnation* was claiming its leader to be a newly-born John Lennon. There were now about as many reincarnated Lennons abroad as there had been freshly-risen Christs in the early Middle Ages.

I stopped in the park to watch the gardeners carefully tending the unsweet soil of the flower-beds, coaxing marigolds and nasturtiums to bloom at least for a few days in the winter, when the sun would not burn them immediately they emerged. The little municipal café was unchanged since British days and still served only icecreams, tea, coffee or soft-drinks, all of them made with non-rationed ingredients and all equally tasteless. Pigeons wandered hopelessly amongst the debris left by customers, occasionally pecking at a piece of wrapping or a sliver of *Sustenance* left behind by some poor devil who had been unable to force his stomach to accept the high-concentrate nutrients we had developed at UNEC for his benefit.

The Cataract's entrance was between pillars which, once stately, Egyptianate and unquestionably European, were now a little the worse for wear, though the gardens on both sides of the drive were heavy with freshly-planted flowers. Bougainvilleas of every brilliant variety covered walls behind avenues of palms leading to a main building the colour of Nile clay, its shutters and ironwork a dark, dignified green, the kind of colour Thomas Cook himself would have picked to represent the security and solid good service which established him as one of the Empire's noblest champions.

I walked into the great lobby cooled by massive carved mahogany punkahs worked on hidden ropes by screened boys. Egypt had had little trouble implementing many of the UN's mandatory energy-saving regulations. She had either carried on as always or had returned, perhaps even with relief, to the days before electricity and gas had become the necessities rather than the luxuries of life.

I crossed the lobby to the wooden verandah where we were to lunch. Georges Abidos was already at our table by the rail looking directly over the empty swimming pool and, beyond that, to the river itself. He was drinking a cup of Lipton's tea and I remarked on it, pointing to the label on the string dangling from his tiny metal pot. "Indeed!" he said. "At ten pounds the pot why shouldn't the Cataract offer us Lipton's, at least!" He dropped his voice. "Though my guess is the teabag has seen more than one customer through the day's heat. Would you like a cup?"

I refused. He hadn't, I said, exactly sold me on the idea. He laughed. He was a small, attractively ugly Greek from Alexandria. Since the flooding, he had been driven, like so many of his fellow citizens to seek work inland. At least half the city had not been thought worth saving as the sea-level had steadily risen to cover it.

"Can't you," he asked, "get your American friends to do something about this new embargo? One misses the cigarettes and I could dearly use a new John B." He indicated his stained Planter's straw and then picked it up to show me the label on the mottled sweatband so that I might verify it was a genuine product of the Stetson Hat Co. of New Jersey. "Size seven and a quarter. But don't get anything here. The Cairo fakes are very close. Very good. But they can't fake the finish, you see."

"I'll remember," I promised. I would send him a Stetson next time I was in the USA.

I felt we had actually conducted our main business before we sat down. The rest of the lunch would be a social affair with someone I had known both professionally and as a close personal acquaintance for many years.

As our mixed *hors d'oeuvres* arrived, Georges Abidos looked with a despairing movement of his mouth out towards the river. "Well,

Paul, have you solved any of our problems?"

"I doubt it," I said. "That's all going on in Majunga now. I'm wondering if my function isn't as some kind of minor smokescreen."

"I thought you'd volunteered."

"Only when they'd decided that one of us had to come. It was a good chance, I thought, to see how my sister was. I had spare relative allowance and lots of energy and travel owing, so I got her a flight out with me. It took forever! But I grew rather worried. The last note I had from her was three months ago and very disjointed. It didn't tell me anything. I'd guessed that her husband had turned up. It was something she said. That's about all I know which would frighten her that much. My mistake, it's emerged. Then I wondered if she wasn't pregnant. I couldn't make head or tail of her letters. They weren't like her at all."

"Women are a trial," said Georges Abidos. "My own sister has divorced, I heard. But then," as if to explain it, "they moved to Kuwait." He turned his eyes back to the river which seemed almost to obsess him. "Look at the Nile. An open sewer running through a desert. What has Egypt done to deserve rescue? She gave the world the ancestors who first offered Nature a serious challenge. Should we be grateful for that? From Lake Nasser to Alexandria the river remains undrinkable and frequently unusable. She once replenished the Earth. Now, what with their fertilisers and sprays, she helps poison it." It was as if all the doubts he had kept to himself as a publicity officer were now being allowed to emerge. "I listen to Blue Danube Radio from Vienna. The English station. It's so much more reliable than the World Service. We are still doing less than we could, they say, here in Egypt."

The tables around us had begun to fill with Saudis and wealthy French people in fashionable silk shifts, and the noise level rose so that it was hard for me to hear my acquaintance's soft tones.

We discussed the changing nature of Aswan. He said he would

be glad to get back to Cairo where he had a new job with the Antiquities Department raising money for specific restoration or reconstruction projects.

We had met at the re-opening of the Cairo Opera House in 1989, which had featured the Houston Opera Company's *Porgy and Bess*, but had never become more than casual friends, though we shared many musical tastes and he had an extraordinary knowledge of modern fiction in English. His enthusiasm was for the older writers like Gilchrist or DeLillo, who had been amongst my own favourites at College.

We were brought some wonderfully tasty Grönburgers and I remarked that the cuisine had improved since I was last here. "French management," he told me. "They have one of the best teams outside of Paris. They all came from Nice after the troubles. Lucky for us. I might almost be tempted to stay! Oh, no! I could not. Even for that! Nubian music is an abomination!"

I told him about my sister, how I was unable to find her and how I was beginning to fear the worst. "The police suggested she was mad."

Georges was dismissive of this. "A dangerous assumption at any time, Paul, but especially these days. And very difficult for us to define here, in Egypt, just as justice is at once a more brutal and a subtler instrument in our interpretation. We never accepted, thank God, the conventional wisdoms of psychiatry. And madness here, as elsewhere, is defined by the people in power, usually calling themselves the State. Tomorrow those power holders could be overthrown by a fresh dynasty, and what was yesterday simple common sense today becomes irresponsible folly. So I do not like to make hasty judgements or pronounce readily on others' moral or mental conditions—lest, indeed, we inadvertently condemn ourselves." He paused. "They say this was not so under the British, that it was fairer, more predictable. Only real troublemakers and criminals went to jail. Now it isn't as bad as it was when I was a lad. Then anyone was liable to arrest. If it was better under the British, then that is our shame." And he lowered his lips to his wineglass.

We had slipped, almost automatically, into discussing the old, familiar topics. "It's sometimes argued," I said, "that the liberal democracies actually stopped the flow of history. A few hundred years earlier, as feudal states, we would have forcibly Christianised the whole of Islam and changed the entire nature of the planet's power struggle. Indeed, all the more childish struggles might have been well and truly over by now!"

"Or it might have gone the other way," Georges suggested dryly, "if the Moors had reconquered France and Northern Europe. After all, Islam did not bring the world to near-ruin. What has the European way achieved except the threat of death for all?"

I could not accept an argument which had already led to massive conversions to Islam amongst the youth of Europe, America and Democratic Africa, representing a sizeable proportion of the vote. This phenomenon had, admittedly, improved the tenor of world politics, but I still deplored it.

"Oh, you're so thoroughly out of step, my friend." Georges Abidos smiled and patted my arm. "The world's changing!"

"It'll die if we start resorting to mystical Islamic solutions."

"Possibly." He seemed unconcerned. I think he believed us unsaveable.

A little drunk, I let him take me back to the Osiris in a calash. He talked affectionately of our good times, of concerts and plays we had seen in the world's capitals before civilian flight had become so impossibly expensive, of the Gilbert and Sullivan season we had attended in Bangkok, of Wagner in Bayreuth and Britten in Glyndebourne. We hummed a snatch from *Iolanthe* before we parted.

When I got up to my room all the shutters had been drawn back to give the apartment the best of the light. I recognised the subtle perfume even as my sister came out of the bathroom to laugh aloud at my astonishment.

11 : Saw Life to Be A Sea Green Dream

Beatrice had cut her auburn hair short and her skin was paler than I remembered. While her blue eyes and red lips remained striking, she had gained an extra beauty. I was overjoyed. This was the opposite of what I had feared to find.

As if she read my mind, she smiled. "Were you expecting the Mad Woman of Aswan?" She wore a light blue cotton skirt and a darker blue shirt.

"You've never looked better." I spoke the honest truth.

She took both my hands in hers and kissed me. "I'm sorry I didn't write. It began to seem such as sham. I *couldn't* write for a while. I got your letters today, when I went to the post office. What a coincidence, I thought—my first sally into the real world and here comes good old Paul to help me. If anyone understands reality, you do."

I was flattered and grinned in the way I had always responded to her half-mocking praise. "Well, I'm here to take you back to it, if you want to go. I've got a pass for you on the Cairo plane in four days' time, and from there we can go to Geneva or London or anywhere in the Community."

"That's marvellous," she said. She looked about my shabby sitting room with its cracked foam cushions, its stained tiles. "Is this the best you get at your rank?"

"This is the best for any rank, these days. Most of us don't travel at all and certainly not by plane."

"The schoomers are still going out of Alex, are they?"

"Oh, yes. To Genoa, some of them. Who has the time?"

"That's what I'd thought of, for me. But here you are! What a bit of luck!"

I was immensely relieved. "Oh, Bea. I thought you might be dead—you know, or worse."

"I was selfish not to keep you in touch, but for a while, of course, I couldn't. Then I was out there for so long…"

"At your dig, you mean?"

She seemed momentarily surprised, as if she had not expected me to know about the dig. "Yes, where the dig was. That's right. I can't remember what I said in my letters."

"That you'd made a terrific discovery and that I must come out the first chance I got. Well, I did. This really was the first chance. Am I too late? Have they closed down the project completely? Are you out of funds?"

"Yes," she smiled. "You're too late, Paul. I'm awfully sorry. You must think I've brought you on a wild goose chase."

"Nonsense. That wasn't why I really came. Good Lord, Bea, I care a lot for you!" I stopped, a little ashamed. She was probably in a more delicate condition than she permitted me to see. "And, anyway, I had some perks coming. It's lovely here, still, isn't it? If you ignore the rubbish tips. You know, and the sewage. And the Nile!" We laughed together. "And the rain and the air," she said. "And the sunlight! Oh, Paul! What if this really is the future?"

12 : A Man In the Night Flaking Tombstones

She asked if I would like to take a drive with her beside the evening river and I agreed at once. I was her senior by a year but she had always been the leader, the initiator and I admired her as much as ever.

We went up past the ruins of the Best Western and the Ramada Inn, the only casualties of a shelling attack in '02, when the Green Jihad had attempted to hole the dam and six women had died. We stopped near the abandoned museum and bought a drink from the ice-stall. As I turned, looking out at the river, I saw the new moon, huge and orange, in the cloudless night. A few desultory mosquitoes hung around our heads and were easily fanned away as we continued up the corniche, looking out at the lights from the boats, the flares on the far side, the palms waving in the soft breeze from the North.

"I'm quitting my job," she said. "I resigned, in fact, months ago. I had a few things to clear up."

"What will you do? Get something in London?"

"Well, I've my money. That was invested very sensibly by Jack before our problems started. Before we split up. And I can do freelance work." Clearly, she was unwilling to discuss the details. "I could go on living here."

"Do you want to?"

"No," she said. "I hate it now. But is the rest of the world any better, Paul?"

"Oh, life's still a bit easier in England. And Italy's all right. And Scandinavia, of course, but that's closed off, as far as residency's concerned. The population's dropping quite nicely in Western Europe. Not everything's awful. The winters are easier."

She nodded slowly as if she were carefully noting each observation. "Well," she said, "anyway, I don't know about Aswan. I'm not sure there's much point in my leaving Egypt. I have a permanent visa, you know."

"Why stay, Bea?"

"Oh, well," she said. "I suppose it feels like home. How's daddy? Is everything all right in Marrakesh?"

"Couldn't be better, I gather. He's having a wonderful time. You know how happy he always was there. And with the new government! Well, you can imagine."

"And mother?"

"Still in London. She has a house to herself in West Hampstead.

Don't ask me how. She's installed the latest EE generators and energy storers. She's got a TV set, a pet option and a gas licence. You know mother. She's always had the right contacts. She'll be glad to know you're OK."

"Yes. That's good, too. I've been guilty of some awfully selfish behavior, haven't I. Well, I'm putting all that behind me and getting on with my life."

"You sound as if you've seen someone. About whatever it was. Have you been ill, Bea?"

"Oh, no. Not really." She turned to reassure me with a quick smile and a hand out to mine, just as always. I nearly sang with relief. "Emotional trouble, you know."

"A boyfriend?"

"Well, yes, I suppose so. Anyway, it's over."

"All the hippies told me you'd been abducted by a flying saucer!"

"Did they?"

I recognised her brave smile. "What's wrong? I hadn't meant to be tactless."

"You weren't. There are so many strange things happening around here. You can't blame people for getting superstitious, can you? After all, we say we've identified the causes, yet can do virtually nothing to find a cure."

"Well, I must admit there's some truth in that. But there are still things we can do."

"Of course there are. I didn't mean to be pessimistic, old Paul." She punched me on the arm and told the driver to let his horse trot for a bit, to get us some air on our faces, since the wind had dropped so suddenly.

She told me she would come to see me at the same time tomorrow and perhaps after that we might go to her new flat. It was only a temporary place while she made up her mind. Why didn't I just go to her there? I said. Because, she said, it was in a maze. You couldn't get a calash through and even the schoolboys would sometimes mislead you by accident. Write it down, I suggested, but she refused with an even broader smile. "You'll see I'm right. I'll take you there tomorrow. There's no mystery. Nothing deliberate."

I went back into the damp, semi-darkness of the Osiris and climbed through black archways to my rooms.

13 : You'll Find No Mirrors In That Cold Abode

I had meant to ask Beatrice about her experience with the Somali woman and the police, but her mood had swung so radically I had decided to keep the rest of the conversation as casual as possible. I went to bed at once more hopeful and more baffled than I had been before I left Cairo.

In the morning I took a cab to the religious academy, or *madrassah*, of the famous Sufi, El Haj Sheik Ibrahim Abu Halil, not because I now needed his help in finding my sister, but because I felt it would have been rude to cancel my visit without explanation. The *madrassah* was out near the old obelisk quarries. Characteristically Moslem, with a tower and a domed mosque, it was reached on foot or by donkey, up a winding, artificial track that had been there for at least two thousand years. I climbed to the top, feeling a little dizzy as I avoided looking directly down into the ancient quarry and saw that the place was built as a series of stone colonnades around a great courtyard with a fountain in it. The fountain, in accordance with the law, was silent.

The place was larger than I had expected and far more casual. People, many obviously drugged, of every age and race sat in groups or strolled around the cloisters. I asked a pale young woman in an Islamic *burqa* where I might find Sheikh Abu Halil. She told me to go to the office and led me as far as a glass door through which I saw an ordinary business layout of pens and paper, mechanical typewriters, acoustic calculators and, impressively, an EMARGY console. I felt as if I were prying. My first job, from which I had resigned, was as an Energy Officer. Essentially the work involved too much peeping-tomism and too little real progress.

A young black man in flared Mouwes and an Afghan jerkin signalled for me to enter. I told him my business and he said, "No problem, man." He asked me to wait in a little room furnished like something still found in any South London dentist's. Even the magazines looked familiar and I did not intend to waste my battery ration plugging in to one. A few minutes later the young man returned and I was escorted through antiseptic corridors to the Sufi's inner sanctum.

I had expected some rather austere sort of Holy Roller's Executive Suite, and was a trifle shocked by the actuality which resembled a scene from *The Arabian Nights.* The Sufi was clearly not celibate, and was an epicurean rather than an aescetic. He was also younger than I had expected. I guessed he was no more than forty-five. Dressed in red silks of a dozen shades, with a massive scarlet turban on his head, he lay on cushions smoking from a silver and brass hookah while behind him on rich, spangled divans, lolled half-a-dozen young women, all of them veiled, all looking at me with frank, if discreet, interest. I felt as if I should apologise for intruding on someone's private sexual fantasy, but the Sufi grinned, beckoned me in, then fell to laughing aloud as he stared into my face. All this, of course, only increased my discomfort. I could see no reason for his amusement.

"You think this a banal piece of play-acting?" He at once became solicitous. "Pardon me, *Herr Doktor.* I misunderstood your expression for a moment. I thought you were an old friend." Now he was almost grave. "How can I help you?"

"Originally," I said, "I was looking for my sister Beatrice. I believe you know her." Was this my sister's secret? Had she involved herself with a charismatic charlatan to whom even I felt drawn? But the banality of it all! True madness, like true evil, I had been informed once, was always characterised by its banality.

"That's it, of course. Becky Bakka was the name the young ones used. She is a very good friend of mine. Are you looking for her no longer, Dr. Bakka?"

I pointed out that von Bek was the family name. The hippies had not made an enormously imaginative leap.

"Oh, the children! Don't they love to play? They are blessed. Think how few of us in the world are allowed by God to play."

"Thou art most tolerant indeed, sidhi." I used my best classical Arabic, at which he gave me a look of considerable approval and addressed me in the same way.

"Doth God not teach us to tolerate, but not to imitate, all the ways of mankind? Are we to judge God, my compatriot?" He had done me the honour, in his own eyes, of addressing me as a coreligionist. When he smiled again his expression was one of benign happiness. "Would you care for some coffee?" he asked in educated English. "Some cakes and so on? Yes, of course." And he clapped his hands, whispering instructions to the nearest woman who rose and left. I was so thoroughly discomforted by this outrageously old-fashioned sexism which, whatever their private practices, few sophisticated modern Arabs were willing to admit to, that I remained silent.

"And I trust that you in turn will tolerate my stupid self-indulgence," he said. "It is a whim of mine—and these young women—to lead the life of Haroun-el-Raschid, eh? Or the great chiefs who ruled in the days before the Prophet. We are all nostalgic for that, in Egypt. The past, you know, is our only escape. You don't begrudge it us, do you?"

I shook my head, although by training and temperament I could find no merit in his argument. "These are changing times," I said. "Your past is crumbling away. It's difficult to tell good from evil or right from wrong, let alone shades of intellectual preference."

"But I can tell you really do still think there are mechanical solutions to our ills."

"Don't you, sidhi?"

"I do. I doubt though that they're much like a medical man's."

"I'm an engineer, not a doctor of medicine."

"Pardon me. It's my day for gaffs, eh? But we're all guilty of making the wrong assumptions sometimes. Let us open the shutters and enjoy some fresh air." Another of the women went to fold back the tall wooden blinds and let shafts of sudden sunlight down upon the maroons, burgundies, dark pinks, bottle-greens and royal blues of that luxurious room. The woman sank into the shadows and only Sheik Abu Halil remained with half his face in light, the other in shade, puffing on his pipe, his silks rippling as he moved a lazy hand. "We are blessed with a marvellous view."

From where we sat it was possible to see the Nile, with its white sails and flanking palms, on the far side of an expanse of glaring granite.

"My sister—" I began.

"A remarkable woman. A saint, without doubt. We have tried to help her, you know."

"I believe you're responsible for getting her out of police custody, sidhi."

"God has chosen her and has blessed her with unusual gifts. Dr. von Bek, we are merely God's instruments. She has brought a little relief to the sick, a little consolation to the despairing."

"She's coming home with me. In three days."

"A great loss for Aswan. But perhaps she's more needed out there. Such sadness, you know. Such deep sadness." I was not sure if he described my sister or the whole world. "In Islam, you see," an ironic twitch of the lip, "we share our despair. It is a democracy of misery." And he chuckled. "This is blasphemy I know, in the West. Especially in America."

"Well, in parts of the North maybe." I smiled. My father was from Mississippi and settled first in Morocco, then in England after he came out of the service. He said he missed the old, bitter-sweet character of the U.S. South. The New South, optimistic and, in his view, Yankified, no longer felt like home. He was more in his element in pre-Thatcher Britain. When she, too, began a programme of "Yankification" of her own he retreated into fantasy, leaving my mother and going to live in a working-class street in a run-down North Eastern town where he joined the Communist Party and demonstrated against closures in the mining, fishing and steel industries. My mother hated it when his name appeared in the papers or, worse in her view, when he wrote intemperate letters to the weekly journals or the heavy dailies. But "Jim Beck" was a contributor to *Marxism Today* and, later, *Red is Green* during his brief flirtation with Trotskyist Conservationism. He gave that up for anarcho-socialism and disappeared completely into the world of the abstract. He now wrote me letters describing the "Moroccan experiment" as the greatest example of genuinely radical politics in action. I had never completely escaped the tyranny of his impossible ideals. This came back to me, there and then, perhaps because in some strange way I found this sufi as charming as I had once found my father. "We say that misery loves company. Is that the same thing?" I felt I was in some kind of awful contest. "Is that why she wanted to stay with you?"

"I knew her slightly before it all changed for her. Afterwards, I knew her better. She seemed very delicate. She came back to Aswan, then went out to the dig a couple more times, then back here. She was possessed of a terrible restlessness she would allow nobody here to address and which she consistently denied. She carried a burden, Dr. von Bek." He echoed the words of Inspector el-Bayoumi. "But perhaps we, even we, shall never know what it was."

14 : On Every Hand—
The Red Collusive Stain

She arrived at the Osiris only a minute or two late. She wore a one-piece worksuit and a kind of bush-hat with a veil. She also carried a briefcase which she displayed in some embarrassment. "Habit, I suppose. I don't need the maps or the notes. I'm taking you into the desert, Paul. Is that OK?"

"We're not going to your place?"

"Not now."

I changed into more suitable clothes and followed her down to the street. She had a calash waiting which carried us to the edge of town, to a camel camp where, much to my dismay, we transferred to grumbling dromedaries. I had not ridden a camel for ten years, but mine proved fairly tractable once we were moving out over the sand.

I had forgotten the peace and the wonderful smell of the desert and it was not long before I had ceased to pay attention to the heat or the motion and had begun to enjoy a mesmeric panorama of dunes and old rock. My sister occasionally used a compass to keep course but sat her high saddle with the confidence of a seasoned drover. We picked up speed until the heat became too intense and we rested under an outcrop of red stone which offered the only shade. It was almost impossible to predict where one would find shade in the desert. A year ago this rock might have been completely invisible beneath the sand; in a few months it might be invisible again.

"The silence is seductive," I said after a while.

My sister smiled. "Well, it whispers to me, these days. But it is wonderful, isn't it? Here you have nothing but yourself, a chance to discover how much of your identity is your own and how much is actually society's. And the ego drifts away. One becomes a virgin beast."

"Indeed!" I found this a little too fanciful for me. "I'm just glad to be away from all that..."

"You're not nervous?"

"Of the desert?"

"Of getting lost. Nothing comes out here, ever, now. Nomads don't pass by and it's been years since a motor vehicle or plane was allowed to waste its ER on mere curiosity. If we died, we'd probably never be found."

"This is a bit morbid, isn't it, Bea? It's only a few hours from Aswan, and the camels are healthy."

"Yes." She rose to put our food and water back into their saddlebags, causing a murmuring and an irritable shifting of the camels. We slept for a couple of hours. Bea wanted to be able to travel at night, when we would make better time under the almost full moon.

The desert at night will usually fill with the noises of the creatures who waken as soon as the sun is down, but the region we next entered seemed as lifeless as the Bical flats, though without their aching mood of desolation. The sand still rose around our camels' feet in silvery gasps and I wrapped myself in the other heavy woolen *gelabea* Beatrice had brought. We slept again, for two or three hours, before continuing on until it was almost dawn and the moon faint and fading in the sky.

"We used to have a gramophone and everything," she said. "We played those French songs mainly. The old ones. And a lot of classic Rai. It was a local collection someone had brought with the machine. You wouldn't believe the mood of camaraderie that was here, Paul. Like Woodstock must have been. We had quite a few young people with us—Egyptian and European mostly—and they all said the same. We felt privileged."

"When did you start treating the sick?" I asked her.

"Treating? Scarcely that! I just helped out with my First Aid kit and whatever I could scrounge from a pharmacy. Most of the problems were easily treated, but not priorities as far as the hospitals are concerned. I did what I could whenever I was in Aswan. But the kits gradually got used and nothing more was sent. After the quake, things began to run down. The Burbank Foundation needed its resources for rebuilding at home."

"But you still do it. Sometimes. You're a legend back there. Ben Achmet told me."

"When I can, I help those nomads cure themselves, that's all. I was coming out here a lot. Then there was some trouble with the police."

"They stopped you? Because of the Somali woman?"

"That didn't stop me." She raised herself in her saddle suddenly. "Look. Can you see the roof there? And the pillars?"

They lay in a shallow valley between two rocky cliffs and they looked in the half-light as if they had been built that very morning. The decorated columns and the massive flat roof were touched a pinkish gold by the rising sun and I could make out hieroglyphics, the blues and ochres of the Egyptian artist. The building, or series of buildings, covered a vast area. "It's a city," I said. I was still disbelieving. "Or a huge temple. My God, Bea! No wonder you were knocked out by this!"

"It's not a city or a temple, in any sense *we* mean." Though she must have seen it a hundred times, she was still admiring of the beautiful stones. "There's nothing like it surviving anywhere else. No record of another. Even this is only briefly mentioned and, as always with Egyptians, dismissively as the work of earlier, less exalted leaders, in this case a monotheistic cult which attempted to set up its own God-king and, in failing, was thoroughly destroyed. Pragmatically, the winners in that contest re-dedicated the place to Sekhmet and then, for whatever reasons—probably economic—abandoned it altogether. There are none of the usual signs of later uses. By the end of Nyusere's reign no more was heard of it at all. Indeed, not much more was heard of Nubia for a long time. This region was never exactly the centre of Egyptian life."

"It was a temple to Ra?"

"Ra, or a sun deity very much like him. The priest here was represented as a servant of the sun. We call the place Onu'us, after him."

"Four thousand years ago? Are you sure this isn't one of those new Dutch repros?" My joke sounded flat, even to me.

"Now you can see why we kept it dark, Paul. It was an observatory, a scientific centre, a laboratory, a library. A sort of university, really. Even the hieroglyphics are different. They tell all kinds of things about the people and the place. And, it had a couple of other functions." Her enthusiasm died and she stopped, dismounting from her camel and shaking sand from her hat. Together we watched the dawn come up over the glittering roof. The pillars, shadowed now, stood only a few feet out of the sand, yet the brilliance of the colour was almost unbelievable. Here was the classic language of the 5th Dynasty, spare, accurate, clean. And it was obvious that the whole place had only recently been refilled. Elsewhere churned, powdery earth and overturned rock spoke of vigorous activity by the discovering team; there was also, on the plain which stretched away from the Southern ridge, a considerable area of fused sand. But even this was now covered by that desert tide which would soon bury again and preserve this uncanny relic.

"You tried to put the sand back?" I felt stupid and smiled at myself.

"It's all we could think of in the circumstances. Now it's far less visible than it was a month ago."

"You sound very proprietorial." I was amused that the mystery should prove to have so obvious a solution. My sister had simply become absorbed in her work. It was understandable that she should.

"I'm sorry," she said. "I must admit..."

For a moment, lost in the profound beauty of the vision, I did not realise she was crying. Just as I had as a little boy, I moved to comfort her, having no notion at all of the cause of her grief, but assuming, I suppose, that she was mourning the death of an important piece of research, the loss of her colleagues, the sheer disappointment at this unlucky end to a wonderful adventure. It was plain, too, that she was completely exhausted.

She drew towards me, smiling an apology. "I want to tell you everything, Paul. And only you. When I have, that'll be it. I'll never mention it again. I'll get on with some sort of life. I'm sick of myself at the moment."

"Bea. You're very tired. Let's go home to Europe where I can coddle you for a bit."

"Perhaps," she said. She paused as the swiftly risen sun outlined sunken buildings and revealed more of a structure lying just below the surface, some dormant juggernaut.

"It's monstrous," I said. "It's the size of the large complex at Luxor. But this is different. All the curved walls, all the circles. Is that to do with sun worship?"

"Astronomy, anyway. We speculated, of course. When we first mapped it on the sonavids. This is the discovery to launch a thousand theories, most of them crackpot. You have to be careful. But it felt to us to be almost a contrary development to what was happening at roughly the same time around Abu Ghurab, although of course there were sun-cults there, too. But in Lower Egypt the gratification and celebration of the Self had reached terrible proportions. All those grandiose pyramids. This place had a mood to it. The more we sifted it out the more we felt it. Wandering amongst those light columns, those open courtyards, was marvellous. All the turquoises and reds and bright yellows. This had to be the centre of some ancient Enlightenment. Far better preserved than Philae, too. And no graffiti carved anywhere, no Christian or Moslem disfigurement. We all worked like maniacs. Chamber after chamber was opened. Gradually, of course, it dawned on us! You could have filled this place with academic people and it would have been a functioning settlement again, just as it was before some petty Pharoah or local governor decided to destroy it. We felt we were taking over from them after a gap of millennia. It gave some of us a weird sense of responsibility. We talked about it. They knew so much, Paul."

"And so little," I murmured. "They only had limited information to work with, Bea..."

"Oh, I think we'd be grateful for their knowledge today." Her manner was controlled, as if she desperately tried to remember how she had once talked and behaved. "Anyway, this is where it all happened. We thought at first we had an advantage. Nobody was bothering to come out to what was considered a very minor find and everyone involved was anxious not to let any government start interfering. It was a sort of sacred trust, if you like. We kept clearing. We weren't likely to be found. Unless we used the emergency radio nobody would waste an energy unit on coming out. Oddly, we found no monumental statuary at all, though the engineering was on a scale with anything from the 19th dynasty—not quite as sophisticated, maybe, but again far in advance of its own time."

"How long did it take you to uncover it all?"

"We never did. We all swore to reveal nothing until a proper international preservation order could be obtained. This government is as desperate for cruise-schoomer dollars as anyone..."

I found myself interrupting her. "This was all covered by hand, Bea?"

"No, no." Again she was amused. "No, the ship did that, mostly. When it brought me back."

A sudden depression filled me. "You mean a spaceship, do you?"

"Yes," she said. "A lot of people here know about them. And I told Di Roper, as well as some of the kids, and the Sufi. But nobody ever believes us—nobody from the real world, I mean. And that's why I wanted to tell you. You're still a real person, aren't you?"

"Bea—you could let me know everything in London. Once we're

back in a more familiar environment. Can't we just enjoy this place for what it is? Enjoy the world for what it is?"

"It's not enjoyable for me, Paul."

I moved away from her. "I don't believe in spaceships."

"You don't believe in much, do you?" Her tone was unusually cool.

I regretted offending her, yet I could not help respond. "The nuts and bolts of keeping this ramshackle planet running somehow. That's what I believe in, Bea. I'm like that chap in the first version of *The African Queen*, only all he had to worry about was a World War and a little beam-engine. Bea, you were here alone and horribly over-tired. Surely...?"

"Let me talk, Paul." There was a note of aching despair in her voice which immediately silenced me and made me lower my head in assent.

We stood there, looking at the sunrise pouring light over that dusty red and brown landscape with its drowned architecture, and I listened to her recount the most disturbing and unlikely story I was ever to hear.

The remains of the team had gone into Aswan for various reasons and Bea was left alone with only a young Arab boy for company. Ali worked as a general servant and was as much part of the team as anyone else, with as much enthusiasm. "He, too, understood the reasons for saying little about our work. Phil Springfield had already left to speak to some people in Washington and Professor al-Bayumi, no close relative of the inspector, was doing what he could in Cairo, though you can imagine the delicacy of his position. Well, one morning, when I was cleaning the dishes and Ali had put a record on the gramophone, this freak storm blew up. It caused a bit of panic, of course, though it was over in a minute or two. And when the sand settled again there was the ship—there, on that bluff. You can see where it came and went."

The spaceship, she said, had been a bit like a flying saucer in that it was circular, with deep sides and glowing horizontal bands at regular intervals. "It was more drum-shaped, though there were discs—I don't know, they weren't metal, but seemed like visible electricity, sort of protruding from it, half on the inside, half on the outside. Much of that moved from a kind of hazy gold into a kind of silver. There were other colours, too. And, I think, sounds. It looked a bit like a kid's tambourine—opaque, sparkling surfaces top and bottom—like the vellum on a drum. And the sides went dark sometimes. Polished oak. The discs, the flange things, went scarlet. They were its main information sensors."

"It was organic?"

"It was a bit. You'd really have to see it for yourself. Anyway, it stood there for a few minutes and then these figures came out. I thought they were test-pilots from that experimental field in Libya and they'd made an emergency landing. I was going to offer them a cup of tea when I realised they weren't human. They had dark bodies that weren't suits exactly but an extra body you wear over your own. Well, you've seen something like it. We all have. It's Akhnatan and Nefertiti. Those strange abdomens and elongated heads, their hermaphroditic quality. They spoke a form of very old-fashioned English. They apologised. They said they had had an instrument malfunction and had not expected to find anyone here. They were prepared to take us with them, if we wished to go. I gathered that these were standard procedures for them. We were both completely captivated by their beauty and the wonder of the event. I don't think Ali hesitated any more than I. I left a note for whomever returned, saying I'd had to leave in a hurry and didn't know when I'd be back. Then we went with them."

"You didn't wonder about their motives?"

"Motives? Yes, Paul, I suppose hallucinations have motives. We weren't the only Earth-people ever to go. Anyway, I never regretted the decision. On the dark side of the Moon the main ship was waiting. That's shaped like a gigantic dung-beetle. You'll laugh when I tell you why. I still find it funny. They're furious because their bosses won't pay for less antiquated vessels. Earth's not a very important project. The ship was designed after one of the first organisms they brought back from Earth, to fit in with what they thought was a familiar form. Apparently their own planet has fewer species but many more different sizes of the same creature. They haven't used the main ship to visit Earth since we began to develop sensitive detection equipment. Their time is different, anyway, and they still find our ways of measuring and recording it very hard to understand."

"They took you to their planet?" I wanted her story to be over. I had heard enough to convince me that she was in need of immediate psychiatric help.

"Oh, no. They've never been there. Not the people I know. Others have been back, but we never communicated with them. They have an artificial environment on Mercury." She paused, noticing my distress. "Paul, you know me. I hated that von Daniken stuff. It was patently rubbish. Yet this was, well, horribly like it. Don't think I wasn't seriously considering I might have gone barmy. When people go mad, you know, they get such ordinary delusions. I suppose they reflect our current myths and apocrypha. I felt foolish at first. Then, of course, the reality grew so vivid, so absorbing, I forgot everything. I could not have run away, Paul. I just walked into it all and they let me. I'm not sure why, except they know things—even circumstances, if you follow me—and must have felt it was better to let me. They hadn't wanted to go underwater and they'd returned to an old location in the Sahara. They'd hoped to find some spares, I think. I know it sounds ridiculously prosaic.

"Well, they took us with them to their base. If I try to pronounce their language it somehow sounds so ugly. Yet it's beautiful. I think in their atmosphere it works. I can speak it Paul. They can speak our languages, too. But there's no need for them. Their home-planet's many light-years beyond the Solar System which is actually very different to Earth, except for some colours and smells, of course. Oh, it's so lovely there, at their base. Yet they complain all the time about how primitive it is and long for the comforts of home. You can imagine what it must be like.

"I became friends with a Reen. He was exquisitely beautiful. He wasn't really a he, either, but an androgyne or something similar. There's more than one type of fertilisation, involving several people, but not always. I was completely taken up with him. Maybe he wasn't so lovely to some human eyes, but he was to mine. He was golden-pale and looked rather negroid, I suppose, like one of those beautiful Masai carvings you see in Kenya, and his shape wasn't altogether manlike, either. His abdomen was permanently rounded—most of them are like that, though in the intermediary sex I think there's a special function. My lover was of that sex, yet he found it impossible to make me understand how he was different. Otherwise they have a biology not dissimilar to ours, with similar organs and so on. It was not hard for me to adapt. Their food is delicious, though they moan about that, too. It's sent from home. Where they can grow it properly. And they have extraordinary music. They have recordings of English TV and radio—and other kinds of recordings, too. Earth's an entire department, you see. Paul," she paused as if regretting the return of the memory, "they have recordings of events. Like battles and ceremonies and architectural stuff. He—my lover—found me an open-air concert at which Mozart was playing. It was too much for me. An archaeologist, and I hadn't the nerve to look at the past as it actually was. I might have got round to it. I meant to. I'd planned to force myself, you know, when I settled down there."

"Bea, don't you know how misanthropic and nuts that sounds?"

"They haven't been 'helping' us or anything like that. It's an observation team. We're not the only planet they're keeping an eye on. They're academics and scientists like us." She seemed to be making an effort to convince me and to repeat the litany of her own faith, whatever it was that she believed kept her sane. Yet the creatures she described, I was still convinced, were merely the inventions of an overtaxed, isolated mind. Perhaps she had been trapped somewhere underground?

"I could have worked there, you see. But I broke the rules."

"You tried to escape?" Reluctantly I humoured her.

"Oh, no!" Her mind had turned backward again and I realised then that it was not any far-off interstellar world but her own planet that had taken her reason. I was suddenly full of sorrow.

"A flying saucer, Bea!" I hoped that my incredulity would bring her back to normality. She had been so ordinary, so matter-of-fact, when we had first met.

"Not really," she said. "The hippies call them Reens. They don't know very much about them, but they've made a cult of the whole thing. They've changed it. Fictionalised it. I can see why that would disturb you. They've turned it into a story for their own purposes. And Sheikh Abu Halil's done the same, really. We've had arguments. I can't stand the exploitation, Paul."

"That's in the nature of a myth." I spoke gently, feeling foolish and puny as I stood looking down on that marvellous construction. I wanted to leave, to return to Aswan, to get us back to Cairo and from there to the relative sanity of rural Oxfordshire, to the village where we had lived with our aunt during our happiest years. She nodded her head. "That's why I stopped saying anything.

"You can't imagine how hurt I was at first, how urgent it seemed to talk about it. I still thought I was only being taught a lesson and they'd return for me. It must be how Eve felt when she realised God wasn't joking." She smiled bitterly at her own naiveté, her eyes full of old pain. "I was there for a long time, I thought, though when I got back it had only been a month or two and it emerged that nobody had ever returned here from Aswan. There had been that Green Jihad trouble and everyone was suddenly packed off back to Cairo and from there, after a while, to their respective homes. People assumed the same had happened to me. If only it had! But really Paul I wouldn't change it."

I shook my head. "I think you were born in the wrong age, Bea. You should have been a priestess of Amon, maybe. Blessed by the Gods."

"We asked them in to breakfast, Ali and me." Shading her eyes against the sun, she raised her arm to point. "Over there. We had a big tent we were using for everything while the others were away. Our visitors didn't think much of our C-Ral and offered us some of their own rations which were far tastier. It was just a scout, that ship. I met my lover later. He had a wonderful sense of irony. As he should, after a thousand years on the same shift."

I could bear no more of this familiar modern apocrypha. "Bea. Don't you think you just imagined it? After nobody returned, weren't you anxious? Weren't you disturbed?"

"They weren't away long enough. I didn't know they weren't coming back, Paul. I fell in love. That wasn't imagination. Gradually, we found ourselves unable to resist the mutual attraction. I suppose I regret that." She offered me a sidelong glance I might have thought cunning in someone else. "I don't blame you for not believing it. How can I prove I'm sane? Or that I was sane then?"

I was anxious to assure her of my continuing sympathy. "You're not a liar, Bea. You never were."

"But you think I'm crazy." All at once her voice became more urgent. "You know how terribly dull madness can be. How conventional most delusions are. You never think you could go mad like that. Then maybe it happens. The flying saucers come down and take you off to Venus, or paradise, where war and disease and atmospheric disintegration are long forgotten. You fall in love with a Venusian. Sexual intercourse is forbidden. You break the law. You're cast out of

Paradise. You can't have a more familiar myth than that, can you, Paul?" Her tone was disturbing. I made a movement with my hand, perhaps to silence her.

"I loved him," she said. "And then I watched the future wither and fade before my eyes. I would have paid any price, done anything, to get back."

That afternoon, as we returned to Aswan, I was full of desperate, bewildered concern for a sister I knew to be in immediate need of professional help. "We'll sort all this out," I reassured her, "maybe when we get to Geneva. We'll see Frank."

"I'm sorry, Paul." She spoke calmly. "I'm not going back with you. I realised it earlier, when we were out at the site. I'll stay in Aswan, after all."

I resisted the urge to turn away from her, and for a while I could not speak.

15 : Whereat Serene And Undevoured He Lay...

The flight was leaving in two days and there would be no other ticket for her. After she went off, filthy and withered from the heat, I rather selfishly used my whole outstanding water allowance and bathed for several hours as I tried to separate the truth from the fantasy. I thought how ripe the world was for Bea's revelation, how dangerous it might be. I was glad she planned to tell no one else, but would she keep to that decision? My impulse was to leave, to flee from the whole mess before Bea started telling me how she had become involved in black magic. I felt deeply sorry for her and I felt angry with her for not being the strong leader I had looked up to all my life. I knew it was my duty to get her back to Europe for expert attention.

"I'm not interested in proving what's true or false, Paul," she had said after agreeing to meet me at the Osiris next morning. "I just want you to *know*. Do you understand?"

Anxious not to upset her further, I had said that I did.

That same evening I went to find Inspector el-Bayoumi in his office. He put out his cigarette as I came in, shook hands and, his manner both affable and relaxed, offered me a comfortable leather chair. "You've found your sister, Mr. von Bek. That's excellent news."

I handed him a "purse" I had brought and told him, in the convoluted manner such occasions demand, that my sister was refusing to leave, that I had a ticket for her on a flight and that it was unlikely I would have a chance to return to Aswan in the near future. If he could find some reason to hold her and put her on the plane, I would be grateful.

With a sigh of regret—at my folly, perhaps—he handed back the envelope. "I couldn't do it, Mr. von Bek, without risking the peace of Aswan, which I have kept pretty successfully for some years. We have a lot of trouble with Green Jihad, you know. I am very short-staffed as a result. You must convince her, my dear sir, or you must leave her here. I assure you, she is much loved and respected. She is a woman of considerable substance and will make her own decisions. I promise, however, to keep you informed."

"By the mail packet? I thought you wanted me to get her out of here!"

"I had hoped you might *persuade* her, Mr. von Bek."

I apologised for my rudeness. "I appreciate your concern, Inspector." I put the money back in my pocket and went out to the corniche, catching the first felucca across to the West Bank where this time I paid off my guides before I reached the English House.

The roses were still blooming around the great brick manor and Lady Roper was cutting some of them, laying them carefully in her bucket. "Really, Paul, I don't think you must worry, especially if she doesn't want to talk about her experiences. *We* all know she's telling the truth. Why don't you have a man to man with Bernie? There he is, in the kitchen."

Through the window, Sir Bernard waved with his cocoa cup before making a hasty and rather obvious retreat.

16 : Your Funeral Bores Them With Its Brilliant Doom

Awaking at dawn the next morning I found it impossible to return to sleep. I got up and tried to make some notes but writing down what my sister had told me somehow made it even more difficult to understand. I gave up. Putting on a cotton *gelabea* and some slippers I went down to the almost empty street and walked to the nearest corner café where I ordered tea and a couple of rolls. All the other little round tables were occupied and from the interior came the sound of a scratched Oum Kal Thoum record. The woman's angelic voice, singing the praises of God and the joys of love, reminded me of my schooldays in Fez, when I had lived with my father during his brief entrepreneurial period, before he had returned to England to become a Communist. Then Oum Kal Thoum had been almost a goddess in Egypt. Now she was as popular again, like so many of the old performers who had left a legacy of 78 rpms which could be played on spring-loaded gramophones or the new clockworks which could also play a delicate LP but which few Egyptians could afford. Most of the records were re-pressed from ancient masters purchased from Athenian studios which, fifty years earlier, had mysteriously manufactured most Arabic recordings. The quality of her voice came through the surface noise as purely as it had once sounded through fractured stereos or on crude pirate tapes in the days of licence and waste. *Inte el Hob*, wistful, celebratory, thoughtful, reminded me of the little crooked streets of Fez, the stink of the dyers and tanners, the extraordinary vividness of the colours, the pungent mint bales, the old men who loved to stand and declaim on the matters of the day with anyone who would listen, the smell of fresh saffron, of lavender carried on the backs of donkeys driven by little boys crying "*balek!*" and insulting, in the vocabulary of a professional soldier, anyone who refused to move aside for them. Life had been sweet then, with unlimited television and cheap air-travel, with any food you could afford and any drink freely available for a few dirhams, and every pleasure in the reach of the common person. The years of Easy, the years of Power, the paradise from which our lazy greed and hungry egos banished us to eternal punishment, to the limbo of the Age of Penury, for which we have only ourselves to blame! But Fez was good, then, in those good, old days.

A little more at peace with myself, I walked down to the river while the muezzin called the morning prayer and I might have been back in the Ottoman Empire, leading the simple, steady life of a small land-owner or a civil servant in the family of the Bey. The debris of the river, the ultimate irony of the Nile filling with all the bottles which had held the water needed because we had polluted the Nile, drew my attention. It was as if the water industry had hit upon a perfect means of charging people whatever they wanted for a drink of *eau naturelle*, while at the same time guaranteeing that the Nile could never again be a source of free water. All this further reinforced my assertion that we were not in the Golden Age those New New Aquarians so longed to recreate. We were in a present which had turned our planet into a single, squalid slum, where nothing beautiful could exist for long, unless in isolation, like Lady Roper's rose garden. We could not bring back the Golden Age. Indeed we were now paying the price of having enjoyed one.

I turned away from the river and went back to the café to find Sheikh Abu Halil sitting in the chair I had recently occupied. "What a coincidence, Mr. von Bek. How are you? How is your wonderful sister?" He spoke educated English.

I suspected for a moment that he knew more than he allowed but then I checked myself. My anxiety was turning into paranoia. This was no way to help my sister.

"I was killing time," he said, "before coming to see you. I didn't want to interrupt your beauty sleep or perhaps even your breakfast, but I guessed aright. You have the habits of Islam." He was flattering me and this in itself was a display of friendship or, at least, affection.

"I've been looking at the rubbish in the river." I shook his hand and sat down in the remaining chair. "There aren't enough police to do anything about it, I suppose."

"Always a matter of economics." He was dressed very differently today in a conservative light and dark blue *gelabea*, like an Alexandrian business man. On his head he wore a discreet, matching cap. "You take your sister back today, I understand, Dr. von Bek."

"If she'll come."

"She doesn't want to go?" The Sufi's eyelid twitched almost raffishly, suggesting to me that he had been awake most of the night. Had he spent that time with Bea?

"She's not sure now," I said. "She hates flying."

"Oh, yes. Flying is a very difficult and unpleasant thing. I myself hate it and would not do it if I could."

I felt he understood far more than that and I was in some way relieved. "You couldn't persuade her of the wisdom of coming with me, I suppose, sidhi?"

"I have already told her what I think, Paul. I think she should go with you. She is unhappy here. Her burden is too much. But she would not and will not listen to me. I had hoped to congratulate you and wish you God Speed."

"You're very kind." I now believed him sincere.

"I love her, Paul." He gave a great sigh and turned to look up at the sky. "She's an angel! I think so. She will come to no harm from us."

"Well—" I was once again at a loss. "I love her too, sidhi. But does she want our love, I wonder?"

"You are wiser than I thought, Paul. Just so. Just so." He ordered coffee and sweetac for us both. "She knows only the habit of giving. She has never learned to receive. Not here, anyway. Especially from you."

"She was always my best friend." I said. "A mother sometimes. An alter-ego. I want to get her to safety, Sheikh Abu Hilal."

"Safety?" At this he seemed sceptical. "It would be good for her to know the normality of family life. She has a husband."

"He's in New Zealand. They split up. He hated what he called her 'charity work'."

"If he was unsympathetic to her calling, that must be inevitable."

"You really think she has a vocation?" The coffee came and the oversweetened breakfast cakes which he ate with considerable relish. "We don't allow these at home. All those chemicals!" There was an element of self-mockery in his manner now that he was away from his *medrassah*. "Yes. We think she has been called. We have many here who believe that of themselves, but most are self-deluding. Aswan is becoming a little over-stocked with mystics and wonder-workers. Eventually, I suppose, the fashion will change, as it did in Nepal, San Francisco or Essaouira. Your sister, however, is special to us. She is so sad, these days, doctor. There is a chance she might find happiness in London. She is spending too long in the desert."

"Isn't that one of the habitual dangers of the professional mystic?" I asked him.

He responded with quiet good humour. "Perhaps of the more old-fashioned type, like me. Did she ever tell you what she passed to Lallah Zenobia that night?"

"You mean the cause of her arrest? Wasn't it money? A purse. The police thought it was."

"But if so, Paul, what was she buying?"

"Peace of mind, perhaps," I said. I asked him if he really believed in people from space, and he said that he did, for he believed that God had created and populated the whole universe as He saw fit. "By the way," he said. "Are you walking up towards the Cataract? There was some kind of riot near there an hour or so ago. The police were involved and some of the youngsters from the holiday villas. Just a peaceful demonstration, I'm sure. That would be nothing to do with your sister?"

I shook my head.

"You'll go back to England, will you, Dr. von Bek?"

"Eventually," I told him. "The way I feel at the moment I might retire. I want to write a novel."

"Oh, your father was a vicar, then?"

I was thoroughly puzzled by this remark. Again he began to laugh. "I do apologise. I've always been struck by the curious fact that so much enduring English literature has sprung, as it were, from the loins of the minor clergy. I wish you luck, Dr. von Bek, in whatever you choose to do. And I hope your sister decides to go with you tomorrow." He kissed me three times on my face. "You both need to discover your own peace. *Sabah el Kher.*"

"*Allah yisabbe'h Kum bil-Kher.*"

The holy man waved a dignified hand as he strolled down towards the corniche to find a calash.

By now the muezzin was calling the mid-morning prayer. I had been away from my hotel longer than planned. I went back through the crowds to the green and white entrance of the Osiris and climbed slowly to my room. It was not in my nature to force my sister to leave and I felt considerably ashamed of my attempt to persuade Inspector el-Bayoumi to extradite her. I could only pray that, in the course of the night, she had come to her senses. My impulse was to seek her out but I still did not know her address.

I spent the rest of the morning packing and making official notes until, at noon, she came through the archway, wearing a blue cotton dress and matching shawl. I hoped this was a sign she was preparing for the flight back to civilisation. "You haven't eaten, have you?" she said.

She had booked a table on the Mut, a floating restaurant moored just below the Cataract. We boarded a thing resembling an Ottoman pleasure barge, all dark green trellises, scarlet fretwork and brass ornament, while inside it was more luxurious than the sufi's "harem". "It's hardly used, of course, these days," Bea said. "Not enough rich people wintering in Aswan any more. But the atmosphere's nice still. You don't mind? It's not against your puritan nature, is it?"

"Only a little." I was disturbed by her apparent normality. We might never have ridden into the desert together, never have talked about aliens and spaceships and Ancient Egyptian universities. I wondered, now, if she were not seriously schizophrenic.

"You do seem troubled, though." She was interrupted by a large man in a dark yellow *gelabea* smelling wildly of garlic who embraced her with affectionate delight. "Beatrice! My Beatrice!" We were introduced. Mustafa shook hands with me as he led us ecstatically to a huge, low table looking over the Nile, where the feluccas and great sailing barges full of holidaymakers came close enough to touch. We sat on massive brocaded foam cushions.

I could not overcome my depression. I was faced with a problem beyond my scope. "You've decided to stay I take it?"

The major domo returned with two large glasses of Campari Soda. "Compliments of the house." It was an extraordinary piece of generosity. We saluted him with our glasses, then toasted each other.

"Yes. She drew her hair over her collar and looked towards the water. "For a while, anyway. I won't get into any more trouble, Paul, I promise. And I'm not the suicide type. That I'm absolutely sure about."

"Good." I would have someone come out to her as soon as possible, a psychiatrist contact in MEDAC who could provide a professional opinion.

"You'll tell me your address?"

"I'm moving. Tomorrow. I'll stay with the Ropers if they'll have me. Any mail care of them will be forwarded. I'm not being deliberately mysterious, dear, I promise. I'm going to write. And meanwhile, I've decided to tell you the whole of it. I want you to remember it, perhaps put it into some kind of shape that I can't. It's important to me that it's recorded. Do you promise?"

I could only promise that I would make all the notes possible.

"Well, there's actually not much else."

I was relieved to know I would not for long have to suffer those miserably banal inventions.

"I fell in love, you see."

"Yes, you told me. With a spaceman."

"We knew it was absolutely forbidden to make love. But we couldn't help ourselves. I mean, with all his self-discipline he was as attracted to me as I was to him. It was important, Paul."

I did my best to give her my full attention while she repeated much of what she had already told me in the desert. There was a kind of Biblical rhythm to her voice. "So they threw me out. I never saw my lover again. I never saw his home again. They brought me back and left me where they had found me. Our tents were gone and everything was obviously abandoned. They let their engines blow more sand over the site. Well, I got to Aswan eventually. I found water and food and it wasn't too hard. I'm not sure why I came here. I didn't know then that I was pregnant. I don't think I knew you could get pregnant. There isn't a large literature on sexual congress with semi-males of the alien persuasion. You'd probably find him bizarre, but for me it was like making love to an angel. All the time. It was virtually our whole existence. Oh, Paul!" She pulled at her collar. She smoothed the table-cloth between her knife and fork. "Well, he was wonderful and he thought I was wonderful. Maybe that's *why* they forbid it. The way they'd forbid a powerful habit-forming stimulant. Do you know I just this second thought of that?"

"That's why you were returned here?" I was still having difficulty following her narrative.

"Didn't I say? Yes. Well, I went to stay with the Ropers for a bit, then I stayed in the commune and then the *medrassah*, but I kept going out to the site. I was hoping they'd relent, you see. I'd have done almost anything to get taken back, Paul."

"To escape from here, you mean?"

"To be with him. That's all. I was—I am—so lonely. Nobody could describe the void."

I was silent, suddenly aware of her terrible vulnerability, still convinced she had been the victim of some terrible deception.

"You're wondering about the child," she said. She put her hand on mine where I fingered the salt. "He was born too early. He lived for eight days. I had him at Lallah Zenobia's. You see, I couldn't tell what he would look like. She was better prepared, I thought. She even blessed him when he was born so that his soul might go to heaven. He was tiny and frail and beautiful. His father's colouring and eyes. My face, I think, mostly. He would have been a *wunderkind*, I shouldn't be surprised. Paul..." Her voice became a whisper. "It was like giving birth to the Messiah."

With great ceremony, our meal arrived. It was a traditional Egyptian *meze* and it was more and better food than either of us had seen in years. Yet we hardly ate.

"I took him back to the site." She looked out across the water again. "I'd got everything ready. I had some hope his father would come to see him. Nobody came. Perhaps it needed that third sex to give him the strength? I waited, but there was not, as the kids say, a Reen to be seen." This attempt at humour was hideous. I took firm hold of her hands. The tears in her eyes were barely restrained.

"He died." She released her hands and looked for something in her bag. I thought for a frightening moment she was going to produce a photograph. "Eight days. He couldn't seem to get enough nourishment from what I was feeding him. He needed that—whatever it was he should have had." She took a piece of linen from her bag and wiped her hands and neck. "You're thinking I should have taken him to the hospital. But this is Egypt, Paul, where people are still arrested for witchcraft and here was clear evidence of my having had congress with an *ifrit.* Who would believe my story? I was aware of what I was doing. I'd never expected the baby to live or, when he did live, to look the way he did. The torso was sort of pear-shaped and there were several embryonic limbs. He was astonishingly lovely. I think he belonged to his father's world. I wish they had come for him. It wasn't fair that he should die."

I turned my attention to the passing boats and controlled my own urge to weep. I was hoping she would stop, for she was, by continuing, hurting herself. But, obsessively, she went on. "Yes, Paul. I could have gone to Europe as soon as I knew I was pregnant and I would have done if I'd had a hint of what was coming, but my instincts told me he would not live or, if he did live, it would be because his father returned for him. I don't think that was self-deception. Anyway, when he was dead I wasn't sure what to do. I hadn't made any plans. Lallah Zenobia was wonderful to me. She said she would dispose of the body properly and with respect. I couldn't bear to have some future archaeologist digging him up. You know, I've always hated that. Especially with children. So I went to her lean-to in Shantytown. I had him wrapped in a shawl—Mother's lovely old Persian shawl—and inside a beautiful inlaid box. I put the box in a leather bag and took it to her."

"That was the Cairene Purse? Or did you give her money, too?"

"Money had nothing to do with it. Do the police still think I was paying her? I offered Zenobia money but she refused. 'Just pray for us all,' was what she said. I've been doing it every night since. The Lord's prayer for everyone. It's the only prayer I know. I learnt it at one of my schools."

"Zenobia went to prison. Didn't you try to tell them she was helping you?"

"There was no point in mentioning the baby, Paul. That would have constituted another crime, I'm sure. She was as good as her word. He was never found. She made him safe somewhere. A little funeral boat on the river late at night, away from all the witnesses, maybe. And they would have found him if she had been deceiving me, Paul. She got him home somehow."

Dumb with sadness, I could only reach out and stroke her arms and hands, reach for her unhappy face.

We ate so as not to offend our host, but without appetite. Above the river the sun was at its zenith and Aswan experienced the familiar, unrelenting light of an African afternoon.

She looked out at the river with its day's flow of debris, the plastic jars, the used sanitary towels, the paper and filth left behind by tourists and residents alike.

With a deep, uneven sigh, she shook her head, folded her arms under her breasts and leaned back in the engulfing foam.

All the *fhouls and* the marinated salads, the *ruqaq* and the meats lay cold before us as, from his shadows, the proprietor observed us with discreet concern.

There came a cry from outside. A boy perched high on the single mast of his boat, his white *gelabea* tangling with his sail so that he seemed all of a piece with the vessel, waved to friends on the shore and pointed into the sky. One of our last herons circled overhead for a moment and then flew steadily south, into what had been the Sudan.

My sister's slender body was moved for a moment by some small, profound anguish.

"He could not have lived here."

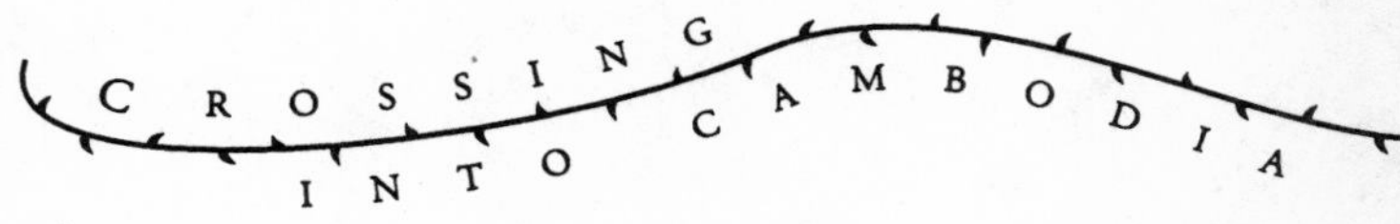
CROSSING
INTO CAMBODIA

Crossing into Cambodia

1

I approached and Savitsky, Commander of the Sixth Division, got up. As usual I was impressed by his gigantic, perfect body. Yet he seemed unconscious either of his power or of his elegance. Although not obliged to do so, I almost saluted him. He stretched an arm towards me. I put the papers into his gloved hand. "These were the last messages we received," I said. The loose sleeve of his Cossack cherkesska slipped back to reveal a battle-strengthened forearm, brown and glowing. I compared his skin to my own. For all that I had ridden with the Sixth for five months, I was still pale; still possessed, I thought, of an intellectual's hands. Evening light fell through the jungle foliage and a few parrots shrieked their last goodnight. Mosquitoes were gathering in the shadows, whirling in tight-woven patterns, like a frightened mob. The jungle smelled of rot. Yakovlev, somewhere, began to play a sad accordion tune.

The Vietnamese spy we had caught spoke calmly from the other side of Savitsky's camp table. "I think I should like to be away from here before nightfall. Will you keep your word, sir, if I tell you what I know?"

Savitsky looked back and I saw the prisoner for the first time (though his presence was of course well known to the camp). His wrists and ankles were pinned to the ground with bayonets but he was otherwise unhurt.

Savitsky drew in his breath and continued to study the documents I had brought him. Our radio was now useless. "He seems to be confirming what these say." He tapped the second sheet. "An attack tonight."

The temple on the other side of the clearing came to life within. Pale light rippled on greenish, half-ruined stonework. Some of our men must have lit a fire there. I heard noises of delight and some complaints from the woman who had been with the spy. One began to shout in that peculiar, irritating high-pitched half-wail they all use when they are trying to appeal to us. For a moment Savitsky and I had a bond in our disgust. I felt flattered. Savitsky made an impatient gesture, as if of embarrassment. He turned his handsome face and looked gravely down at the peasant. "Does it matter to you? You've lost a great deal of blood."

"I do not think I am dying."

Savitsky nodded. He was economical in everything, even his cruelties. He had been prepared to tear the man apart with horses, but he knew that he would tire two already over-worked beasts. He picked up his cap from the camp table and put it thoughtfully on his head. From the deserted huts came the smell of our horses as the wind reversed its direction. I drew my borrowed burka about me. I was the only one in our unit to bother to wear it, for I felt the cold as soon as the sun was down.

"Will you show me on the map where they intend to ambush us?"

"Yes," said the peasant. "Then you can send a man to spy on their camp. He will confirm what I say."

Crossing Into Cambodia

MICHAEL MOORCOCK

I stood to one side while these two professionals conducted their business. Savitsky strode over to the spy and very quickly, like a man plucking a hen, drew the bayonets out and threw them on the ground. With some gentleness, he helped the peasant to his feet and sat him down in the leather campaign chair he had carried with him on our long ride from Danang, where we had disembarked off the troop-ship which had brought us from Vladivostock.

"I'll get some rags to stop him bleeding," I said.

"Good idea," confirmed Savitsky. "We don't want the stuff all over the maps. You'd better be in on this, anyway."

As the liaison officer, it was my duty to knew what was happening. That is why I am able to tell this story. My whole inclination was to return to my billet where two miserable ancients cowered and sang at me whenever I entered or left but where at least I had a small barrier between me and the casual day-to-day terrors of the campaign. But, illiterate and obtuse though these horsemen were, they had accurate instincts and could tell immediately if I betrayed any sign of fear. Perhaps, I thought, it is because they are all so used to disguising their own fears. Yet bravery was a habit with them and I yearned to catch it. I had ridden with them in more than a dozen encounters, helping to drive the Cambodians back into their own country. Each time I had seen men and horses blown to pieces, torn apart, burned alive. I had come to exist on the smell of blood and gun-powder as if it were a substitute for air and food—I identified it with the smell of Life itself—yet I had still failed to achieve that strangely passive sense of inner calm my comrades all, to a greater or lesser degree, displayed.

Only in action did they seem possessed in any way by the outer world, although they still worked with efficient ferocity, killing as quickly as possible with lance, sabre or carbine and, with ghastly humanity, never leaving a wounded man of their own or the enemy's without his throat cut or a bullet in his brain. I was thankful that these, my traditional foes, were now allies for I could not have resisted them had they turned against me.

I bound the peasant's slender wrists and ankles. He was like a child. He said: "I knew there were no arteries cut." I nodded at him. "You're the political officer, aren't you?" He spoke almost sympathetically.

"Liaison," I said.

He was satisfied by my reply, as if I had confirmed his opinion. He added: "I suppose it's the leather coat. Almost a uniform."

I smiled. "A sign of class difference, you think?"

His eyes were suddenly drowned with pain and he staggered, but recovered to finish what he had evidently planned to say. "You Ukranians are natural bourgeoisie. It's not your fault. It's your turn."

Savitsky was too tired to respond with anything more than a small smile. I felt that he agreed with the peasant and that these two excluded me, felt superior to me. I knew anger, then. Tightening the last rag on his left wrist, I made the spy wince. Satisfied that my honour was avenged I cast an eye over the map. "Here we are," I said. We were on the very edge of Cambodia. A small river, easily forded, formed the border. We had heard it just before we had entered this village. Scouts confirmed that it lay no more than half a verst to the west. The stream on the far side of the village, behind the temple, was a tributary.

"You give your word you won't kill me," said the Vietnamese.

"Yes," said Savitsky. He was beyond joking. We all were. It had been ages since any of us had been anything but direct with one another, save for the conventional jests which were merely part of the general noise of the squadron, like the jangling of harness. And he was beyond lying, except where it was absolutely necessary. His threats were as unqualified as his promises.

"They are here." The spy indicated a town. He began to shiver. He was wearing only torn shorts. "And some of them are here, because they think you might use the bridge rather than the ford."

"And the attacking force for tonight?"

"Based here." A point on our side of the river.

Savitsky shouted. "Pavlichenko."

From the Division Commander's own tent, young Pavlichenko, capless, with ruffled fair hair and a look of restrained disappointment, emerged. "Comrade?"

"Get a horse and ride with this man for half-an-hour the way we came today. Ride as fast as you can, then leave him and return to camp."

Pavlichenko ran towards the huts where the horses were stabled. Savitsky had believed the spy and was not bothering to check his information. "We can't attack them," he murmured. "We'll have to wait until they come to us. It's better." The flap of Savitsky's tent was now open. I glanced through and to my surprise saw a Eurasian girl of about fourteen. She had her feet in a bucket of water. She smiled at me. I looked away.

Savitsky said: "He's washing her for me. Pavlichenko's an expert."

"My wife and daughters?" said the spy.

"They'll have to remain now. What can I do?" Savitsky shrugged in the direction of the temple. "You should have spoken earlier."

The Vietnamese accepted this and, when Pavlichenko returned with the horse, leading it and running as if he wished to get the job over with in the fastest possible time, he allowed the young Cossack to lift him onto the saddle.

"Take your rifle," Savitsky told Pavlichenko. "We're expecting an attack."

Pavlichenko dashed for his own tent, the small one close to Savitsky's. The horse, as thoroughly trained as the men who rode him, stood awkwardly but quietly beneath his nervous load. The spy clutched the saddle pommel, the mane, his bare feet angled towards the mount's neck. He stared ahead of him into the night. His wife and daughter had stopped their appalling wailing but I thought I could hear the occasional feminine grunt from the temple. The flames had become more animated. His other daughter, her feet still in the bucket, held her arms tightly under her chest and her curious eyes looked without rancour at her father, then at the Division Commander, then, finally, at me. Savitsky spoke. "You're the intellectual, Bekov. She doesn't know Russian. Tell her that her father will be safe. She can join him tomorrow."

"My Vietnamese might not be up to that."

"Use English or French, then." He began to tidy his maps, calling over Kreshenko, who was in charge of the guard.

I entered the tent and was shocked by her little smile. She had a peculiar smell to her—like old tea and cooked rice. I knew my Vietnamese was too limited so I asked her if she spoke French. She was of the wrong generation. "Amerikanski," she told me. I relayed Savitsky's message. She said: "So I am the price of the old bastard's freedom."

"Not at all." I reassured her. "He told us what we wanted. It was just bad luck for you that he used you three for cover."

She laughed. "Nuts! It was me got him to do it. With my sister. Tao's boyfriend works for the Cambodians." She added: "They seemed to be winning at the time."

Savitsky entered the tent and zipped it up from the bottom. He used a single, graceful movement. For all that he was bone-weary, he moved with the unconscious fluidity of an acrobat. He lit one of his foul-smelling papyrosi and sat heavily on the camp bed beside the girl.

"She speaks English," I said. "She's a half-caste. Look."

He loosened his collar. "Could you ask her if she's clean, comrade?"

"I doubt it," I said. I repeated what she had told me.

He nodded. "Well, ask her if she'll be a good girl and use her mouth. I just want to get on with it. I expect she does, too."

I relayed the D.C.'s message.

"I'll bite his cock off if I get the chance," said the girl.

Outside in the night the horse began to move away. I explained what she had said.

"I wonder, comrade," Savitsky said, "if you would oblige me by holding the lady's head." He began to undo the belt of his trousers, pulling up his elaborately embroidered shirt.

The girl's feet became noisy in the water and the bucket overturned. In my leather jacket, my burka, with my automatic pistol at her right ear, I restrained the girl until Savitsky had finished with her. He began to take off his boots. "Would you care for her yourself?"

I shook my head and escorted the girl from the tent. She was walking in that familiar stiff way women have after they have been raped. I asked her if she was hungry. She agreed that she was. I took her to my billet. The old couple found some more rice and I watched her eat it.

Later that night she moved towards me from where she had been lying more or less at my feet. I thought I was being attacked and shot her in the stomach. Knowing what my comrades would think of me if I tried to keep her alive (it would be a matter of hours) I shot her in the head to put her out of her misery. As luck would have it, these shots woke the camp and when the Khmer soldiers attacked a few moments later we were ready for them and killed a great many before the rest ran back into the jungle. Most of these soldiers were younger than the girl.

In the morning, to save any embarrassment, the remaining women were chased out of the camp in the direction taken by the patriarch. The old couple had disappeared and I assumed that they would not return or, if they did, that they would bury the girl, so I left her where I had shot her. A silver ring she wore would compensate them for their trouble. There was very little food remaining in the village, but what there was we ate for our breakfast or packed into our saddlebags. Then, mounting up, we followed the almost preternaturally handsome Savitsky back into the jungle, heading for the river.

2

When our scout did not return after we had heard a long burst of machine-gun fire, we guessed that he had found at least part of the enemy ambush and that the spy had not lied to us, so we decided to cross the river at a less convenient spot where, with luck, no enemy would be waiting.

The river was swift but had none of the force of Ukranian rivers and Pavlichenko was sent across with a rope which he tied to a tree-trunk. Then we entered the water and began to swim our horses across. Those who had lost the canvas covers for their carbines kept them high in the air, holding the rope with one hand and guiding their horses with legs and with reins which they gripped in their teeth. I was more or less in the middle, with half the division behind me and half beginning to assemble on dry land on the other side, when Cambodian aircraft sighted us and began an attack dive. The aircraft were in poor repair, borrowed from half-a-dozen other countries, and their guns, aiming equipment and, I suspect, their pilots, were in worse condition, but they killed seven of our men as we let go of the ropes, slipped out of our saddles, and swam beside our horses, making for the far bank, while those still on dry land behind us went to cover where they could. A couple of machine-gun carts were turned on the attacking planes, but these were of little use. The peculiar assortment of weapons used against us—tracers, two rockets, a few napalm canisters which struck the water and sank (only one opened and burned but the mixture was quickly carried off by the current) and then they were flying back to base somewhere in Cambodia's interior—indicated that they had very little conventional armament left. This was true of most of the participants at this stage, which is why our cavalry had proved so effective. But they had bought some time for their ground-troops who were now coming in.

In virtual silence, any shouts drowned by the rushing of the river, we crossed to the enemy bank and set up a defensive position, using the machine-gun carts which were last to come across on ropes. The Cambodians hit us from two sides—moving in from their original ambush positions—but we were able to return their fire effectively, even using the anti-tank weapons and the mortar which, hitherto, we had tended to consider useless weight. They used arrows, blow-darts, automatic rifles, pistols and a flame-thrower which only worked for a few seconds and did us no harm. The Cossacks were not happy with this sort of warfare and as soon as there was a lull we had mounted up, packed the gear in the carts, and with sabers drawn were howling into the Khmer Stalinists (as we had been instructed to term them). Leaving them scattered and useless, we found a bit of concrete road along which we could gallop for a while. We slowed to a trot and then to a walk. The pavement was potholed and only slightly less dangerous than the jungle floor. The jungle was behind us now and seemed to have been a screen hiding the devastation ahead. The landscape was virtually flat, as if it had been bombed clean of contours, with a few broken buildings, the occasional blackened tree, and ash drifted across the road, coming sometimes up to our horses' knees. The ash was stirred by a light wind. We had witnessed scenes like it before, but never on such a scale. The almost colourless nature of the landscape was emphasized by the unrelieved brilliance of the blue sky overhead. The sun had become very hot.

Once we saw two tanks on the horizon, but they did not challenge us. We continued until early afternoon when we came to the remains of some sort of modern power installation and we made camp in the shelter of its walls. The ash got into our food and we drank more of our water than was sensible. We were all covered in the grey stuff by this time.

"We're like corpses," said Savitsky. He resembled an heroic statue of the sort which used to be in almost every public square in the Soviet Union. "Where are we going to find anything to eat in this?"

"It's like the end of the world," I said.

"Have you tried the radio again?"

I shook my head. "It isn't worth it. Napalm eats through wiring faster than it eats through you."

He accepted this and with a naked finger began to clean off the inner rims of the goggles he (like most of us) wore as protection against sun, rain and dust. "I could do with some orders," he said.

"We were instructed to move into the enemy's territory. That's what we're doing."

"Where, we were told, we would link up with American and Australian mounted units. Those fools can't ride. I don't know why they ever thought of putting them on horses. Cowboys!"

I saw no point in repeating an already stale argument. It was true, however, that the Western cavalry divisions found it hard to match our efficient savagery. I had been amused, too, when they had married us briefly with a couple of Mongolian squadrons. The Mongols had not ridden to war in decades and had become something of a laughing stock with their ancient enemies, the Cossacks. Savitsky believed that we were the last great horsemen. Actually, he did not include me; for I was a very poor rider and not a Cossack, anyway. He thought it was our destiny to survive the War and begin a new and braver civilization: "Free from the influence of women and Jews". He recalled the great days of the Zaphorozhian Sech, from which women had been forbidden. Even amongst the Sixth he was regarded as something of a conservative. He continued to be admired more than his opinions.

When the men had watered our horses and replaced the water bags in the cart, Savitsky and I spread the map on a piece of concrete and found our position with the help of the compass and sextant (there were no signs or landmarks). "I wonder what has happened to

Angkor," I said. It was where we were supposed to meet other units, including the Canadians to whom, in the months to come, I was to be attached (I was to discover later that they had been in our rear all along).

"You think it's like this?" Savitsky gestured. His noble eyes began to frown. "I mean, comrade, would you say it was worth our while making for Angkor now?"

"We have our orders," I said. "We've no choice. We're expected."

Savitsky blew dust from his mouth and scratched his head. "There's about half our division left. We could do with reinforcements. Mind you, I'm glad we can see a bit of sky at last." We had all felt claustrophobic in the jungle.

"What is it, anyway, this Angkor? Their capital?" he asked me.

"Their Stalingrad, maybe."

Savitsky understood. "Oh, it has an importance to their morale. It's not strategic?"

"I haven't been told about its strategic value."

Savitsky, as usual, withdrew into his diplomatic silence, indicating that he did not believe me and thought that I had been instructed to secrecy. "We'd best push on," he said. "We've a long way to go, eh?"

After we had mounted up, Savitsky and I rode side by side for a while, along the remains of the concrete road. We were in some way ahead of the long column, with its riders, its baggage-waggons, and its Makhno-style machine-gun carts. We were sitting targets for any planes and, because there was no cover, Savitsky and his men casually ignored the danger. I had learned not to show my nervousness but I was not at that moment sure how well hidden it was.

"We are the only vital force in Cambodia," said the Division Commander with a beatific smile. "Everything else is dead. How these yellow bastards must hate one another." He was impressed, perhaps admiring.

"Who's to say?" I ventured. "We don't know who else has been fighting. There isn't a nation now that's not in the War."

"And not one that's not on its last legs. Even Switzerland." Savitsky gave a superior snort. "But what an inheritance for us!"

I became convinced that, quietly, he was going insane.

3

We came across an armoured car in a hollow, just off the road. One of our scouts had heard the crew's moans. As Savitsky and I rode up, the scout was covering the uniformed Khmers with his carbine, but they were too far gone to offer us any harm.

"What's wrong with 'em?" Savitsky asked the scout.

The scout did not know. "Disease," he said. "Or starvation. They're not wounded."

We got off our horses and slid down into the crater. The car was undamaged. It appeared to have rolled gently into the dust and become stuck. I slipped into the driving seat and tried to start the engine, but it was dead. Savitsky had kicked one of the wriggling Khmers in the genitals but the man did not seem to notice the pain much, though he clutched himself, almost as if he entered into the spirit of a ritual. Savitsky was saying "Soldiers. Soldiers", over and over again. It was one of the few Vietnamese words he knew. He pointed in different directions, looking with disgust on the worn-out men. "You'd better question them," he said to me.

They understood my English, but refused to speak it. I tried them in French. "What happened to your machine?"

The man Savitsky had kicked continued to lie on his face, his arms stretched out along the ashy ground towards us. I felt he wanted to touch us: to steal our vitality. I felt sick as I put the heel of my boot on his hand. One of his comrades said: "There's no secret to it. We ran out of essence." He pointed to the armoured car. "We ran out of essence."

"You're a long way from your base."

"Our base is gone. There's no essence anywhere."

I believed him and told Savitsky who was only too ready to accept this simple explanation.

As usual, I was expected to dispatch the prisoners. I reached for my holster, but Savitsky, with rare sympathy, stayed my movement. "Go and see what's in that can," he said, pointing. As I waded towards the punctured metal, three shots came from the Division Commander's revolver. I wondered at his mercy. Continuing with this small farce, I looked at the can, held it up, shook it, and threw it back into the dust. "Empty," I said.

Savitsky was climbing the crater towards his horse. As I scrambled behind him he said: "It's the Devil's world. Do you think we should give ourselves up to Him?"

I was astonished by this unusual cynicism.

He got into his saddle. Unconsciously, he assumed the pose, often seen in films and pictures, of the noble revolutionary horseman—his head lifted, his palm shielding his eyes as he peered towards the West.

"We seem to have wound up killing Tatars again," he said with a smile as I got clumsily onto my horse. "Do you believe in all this history, comrade?"

"I've always considered the theory of precedent absolutely infantile," I said.

"What's that?"

I began to explain, but he was already spurring forward, shouting to his men.

4

On the third day we had passed through the ash-desert and our horses could at last crop at some grass on the crest of a line of low hills which looked down on glinting, misty paddy-fields. Savitsky, his field-glasses to his eyes, was relieved. "A village," he said. "Thank god. We'll be able to get some provisions."

"And some exercise," said Pavlichenko behind him. The boy laughed, pushing his cap back on his head and wiping grimy sweat from his brow. "Shall I go down there, comrade?" Savitsky agreed, telling Pavlichenko to take two others with him. We watched the Cossacks ride down the hill and begin cautiously to wade their horses through the young rice. The sky possessed a greenish tinge here, as if it reflected the fields. It looked like the Black Sea lagoons at midsummer. A smell of foliage, almost shocking in its unfamiliarity, floated up to us. Savitsky was intent on watching the movements of his men, who had unslung their carbines and dismounted as they reached the village. With reins looped on their arms they moved slowly in, firing a few experimental rounds at the huts. One of them took a dummy grenade from his saddle-bag and threw it into a nearby doorway. Peasants, already starving to the point of death it seemed, ran out. The young Cossacks ignored them, looking for soldiers. When they were satisfied that the village was clear of traps, they waved us in. The peasants began to gather together at the centre of the village. Evidently they were used to this sort of operation.

While our men made their thorough search I was again called upon to perform my duty and question the inhabitants. These, it emerged, were almost all intellectuals, part of an old Khmer Rouge re-education programme (virtually a sentence of death by forced labour). It was easier to speak to them but harder to understand their complicated answers. In the end I gave up and, made impatient by the whining appeals of the wretches, ignored them. They knew nothing of use to us. Our men were disappointed in their expectations. There were only old people in the village. In the end they took the least aged of the women off and had them in what had once been some sort of administration hut. I wondered at their energy. It occurred to me that this was something they expected of one another and that they would lose face if they did not perform the necessary actions. Eventually, when we had eaten what we could find, I returned to questioning two of the old men. They were at least antagonistic to the Cambodian troops and were glad to tell us anything they could. However, it seemed there had been no large movements in the area. The occasional plane or helicopter had gone over a few days earlier. These were probably part of the flight which had attacked us at the river. I asked if they had any news of Angkor, but there was no radio here and they expected us to know more than they did. I pointed towards the purple hills on the other side of the valley. "What's over there?"

They told me that as far as they knew it was another valley, similar to this but larger. The hills looked steeper and were wooded. It would be a difficult climb for us unless there was a road. I got out the map. There was a road indicated. I pointed to it. One of the old men nodded. Yes, he thought that road was still there, for it led, eventually, to this village. He showed me where the path was. It was rutted where, some time earlier, heavy vehicles had been driven along it. It disappeared into dark, green, twisting jungle. All the jungle meant to me now was mosquitoes and a certain amount of cover from attacking planes.

Careless of leeches and insects, the best part of the division was taking the chance of a bath in the stream which fed the paddy-fields. I could not bring myself to strip in the company of these healthy men. I decided to remain dirty until I had the chance of some sort of privacy.

"I want the men to rest," said Savitsky. "Have you any objection to our camping here for the rest of today and tonight?"

"It's a good idea," I said. I sought out a hut, evicted the occupants, and went almost immediately to sleep.

In the morning I was awakened by a trooper who brought me a

metal mug full of the most delicately scented tea. I was astonished and accepted it with some amusement. "There's loads of it here," he said. "It's all they've got!"

I sipped the tea. I was still in my uniform, with the burka on the ground beneath me and my leather jacket folded for a pillow. The hut was completely bare. I was used to noticing a few personal possessions and began to wonder if they had hidden their stuff when they had seen us coming. Then I remembered that they were from the towns and had been brought here forcibly. Perhaps now, I thought, the war would pass them by and they would know peace, even happiness, for a bit. I was scratching my ear and stretching when Savitsky came in, looking grim. "We've found a damned burial ground," he said. "Hundreds of bodies in a pit. I think they must be the original inhabitants. And one or two soldiers—at least, they were in uniform."

"You want me to ask what they are?"

"No! I just want to get away. God knows what they've been doing to one another. They're a filthy race. All grovelling and secret killing. They've no guts."

"No soldiers, either," I said. "Not really. They've been preyed on by bandits for centuries. Bandits are pretty nearly the only sort of soldiers they've ever known. So the ones who want to be soldiers emulate them. Those who don't want to be soldiers treat the ones who do as they've always treated bandits. They are conciliatory until they get a chance to turn the tables."

He was impressed by this. He rubbed at a freshly-shaven chin. He looked years younger, though he still had the monumental appearance of a god. "Thieves, you mean. They have the mentality of thieves, their soldiers?"

"Aren't the Cossacks thieves?"

"That's foraging." He was not angry. Very little I said could ever anger him because he had no respect for my opinions. I was the necessary political officer, his only link with the higher, distant authority of Kiev, but he did not have to respect my ideas any more than he respected those which came to him from Moscow. What he respected there was the power and the fact that in some way Ukraine was mystically represented in our leaders. "We leave in ten minutes," he said.

I noticed that Pavlichenko had polished his boots for him.

By that afternoon, after we had crossed the entire valley on an excellent dirt road through the jungle and had reached the top of the next range of hills, I had a pain in my stomach. Savitsky noticed me holding my hands against my groin and said laconically, "I wish the doctor hadn't been killed. Do you think it's typhus?" Naturally, it was what I had suspected.

"I think it's just the tea and the rice and the other stuff. Maybe mixing with all the dust we've swallowed." He looked paler than usual. "I've got it, too. So have half the others. Oh, shit!"

It was hard to tell, in that jungle at that time of day, if you had a fever. I decided to put the problem out of my mind as much as possible until sunset when it would become cooler.

The road began to show signs of damage and by the time we were over the hill and looking down on the other side we were confronting scenery if anything more desolate than that which we had passed through on the previous three days. It was a grey desert, scarred by the broken road and bomb-craters. Beyond this and coming towards us was a wall of dark dust; unmistakably an army on the move. Savitsky automatically relaxed in his saddle and turned back to see our men moving slowly up the wooded hill. "I think they must be marching this way," Savitsky cocked his head to one side. "What's that?"

It was a distant shriek. Then a whole squadron of planes was swooping in low. We could see their crudely-painted Khmer Rouge markings, their battered fuselages. The men began to scatter off the road, but the planes ignored us. They went zooming by, seeming to be fleeing rather than attacking. I looked at the sky, but nothing followed them.

We took our field-glasses from their cases and adjusted them. In the dust I saw a mass of barefoot infantry bearing rifles with fixed bayonets. There were also trucks, a few tanks, some private cars, bicycles, motor-bikes, ox-carts, hand-carts, civilians with bundles. A filthy ooze of defeated soldiers and refugees.

"I think we've missed the action." Savitsky was furious. "We were beaten to it, eh? And by Australians, probably!"

My impulse to shrug was checked. "Damn!" I said a little weakly.

This caused Savitsky to laugh at me. "You're relieved. Admit it!"

I knew that I dare not share his laughter, lest it become hysterical and turn to tears, so I missed a moment of possible comradeship. "What shall we do?" I asked. "Go round them?"

"It would be easy enough to go through them. Finish them off. It would stop them destroying this valley, at least." He did not, by his tone, much care.

The men were assembling behind us. Savitsky informed them of the nature of the rabble ahead of us. He put his field-glasses to his eyes again and said to me: "Infantry, too. Quite a lot. Coming on faster."

I looked. The barefoot soldiers were apparently pushing their way through the refugees to get ahead of them.

"Maybe the planes radioed back," said Savitsky. "Well, it's something to fight."

"I think we should go round," I said. "We should save our strength. We don't know what's waiting for us at Angkor."

"It's miles away yet."

"Our instructions were to avoid any conflict we could," I reminded him.

He sighed. "This is Satan's own country." He was about to give the order which would comply with my suggestion when, from the direction of Angkor Wat, the sky burst into white fire. The horses reared and whinneyed. Some of our men yelled and flung their arms over their eyes. We were all temporarily blinded. Then the dust below seemed to grow denser and denser. We watched in fascination as the dark wall became taller, rushing upon us and howling like a million dying voices. We were struck by the ash and forced onto our knees, then onto our bellies, yanking our frightened horses down with us as best we could. The stuff stung my face and hands and even those parts of my body protected by heavy clothing. Larger pieces of stone rattled against my goggles.

When the wind had passed and we began to stand erect, the sky was still very bright. I was astonished that my field glasses were intact. I put them up to my burning eyes and peered through swirling ash at the Cambodians. The army was running along the road towards us, as terrified animals flee a forest-fire. I knew now what the planes had been escaping. Our Cossacks were in some confusion, but were already regrouping, shouting amongst themselves. A number of horses were still shying and whickering but by and large we were calm again.

"Well, comrade," said Savitsky with a sort of mad satisfaction, "what do we do now? Wasn't that Angkor Wat, where we're supposed to meet our allies?"

I was silent. The mushroom cloud on the horizon was growing. It had the hazy outlines of a gigantic, spreading cedar tree, as if all at once that wasteland of ash had become promiscuously fertile. An aura of bloody red surrounded it, like a silhouette in the sunset. The strong, artificial wind was still blowing in our direction. I wiped dust from my goggles and lowered them back over my eyes. Savitsky gave the order for our men to mount. "Those bastards down there are in our way," he said. "We're going to charge them."

"What?" I could not believe him.

"When in doubt," he told me, "attack."

"You're not scared of the enemy," I said, "but there's the radiation."

"I don't know anything about radiation." He turned in his saddle to watch his men. When they were ready he drew his sabre. They imitated him. I had no sabre to draw.

I was horrified. I pulled my horse away from the road. "Division Commander Savitsky, we're duty-bound to conserve..."

"We're duty-bound to make for Angkor," he said. "And that's what we're doing." His perfect body poised itself in the saddle. He raised his sabre.

"It's not like ordinary dying," I began. But he gave the order to trot forward. There was a rictus of terrifying glee on every mouth. The light from the sky was reflected in every eye.

I moved with them. I had become used to the security of numbers and I could not face their disapproval. But gradually they went ahead of me until I was in the rear. By this time we were almost at the bottom of the hill and cantering towards the mushroom cloud which was now shot through with all kinds of dark, swirling colours. It had become like a threatening hand, while the wind-borne ash stung our bodies and drew blood on the flanks of our mounts.

Yakovlev, just ahead of me, unstrapped his accordion and began to play some familiar Cossack battle-song. Soon they were all singing. Their pace gradually increased. The noise of the accordion died but their song was so loud now it seemed to fill the whole world. They reached full gallop, charging upon that appalling outline, the quintessential symbol of our doom, as their ancestors might have charged the very gates of Hell. They were swift, dark shapes in the dust. The song became a savage, defiant roar.

My first impulse was to charge with them. But then I had turned my horse and was trotting back towards the valley and the border, praying that, if I ever got to safety, I would not be too badly contaminated.

for Nathalie Babel